Who was this Will Thatcher?

"So what is it that intrigues all the girls? His remoteness? Or is he some kind of modern Pied Piper, conceited and unbearable?" Trinity's curiosity was piqued.

Faith's eyes flashed fire. "Absolutely not! I've never known a more unspoiled young man."

She sounded hypnotized by Will Thatcher! It wasn't like Faith to rave about young men. Well, bring on Mr. Ideal. Trinity tossed her proud head. At least one girl wouldn't follow after him like a pathetic lamb. Yet she couldn't help feeling a little pain at the thought of the young man who held his dying brother, powerless to do anything.

COLLEEN L. REECE is a prolific author with over sixty published books. With the popular *Storm Clouds Over Chantel*, Reece established herself as a doyenne of Christian romance.

Books by Colleen L. Reece

HEARTSONG PRESENTS

HP2—Wildflower Harvest

ROMANCE READER—TWO BOOKS IN ONE

RR1—Honor Bound & The Calling of Elizabeth Courtland
RR4—To Love and Cherish & Storm Clouds Over Chantel
RR6—Angel of the North & Legacy of Silver
RR8—A Girl Called Cricket & The Hills of Hope

A Torch
For Trinity

Colleen L. Reece

Heartsong Presents

To all those family members who have gone before me and whose torches lighted the one I carry.

ISBN 1-55748-322-1

A TORCH FOR TRINITY

PRINTED IN U.S.A.

Prologue
Late Summer 1912

She didn't look back. She didn't dare.

Only after the westbound train hurled around a bend and gathered enough momentum that a leap to freedom would mean certain death did fourteen-year-old Trinity Mason unclench her fingers and stare out the window. Her future seemed bleak indeed.

A-way, a-way, taunted the clacking wheels. Trinity's blue eyes darkened to almost black, the same color as the soft waves framing a delicate complexion that even the hottest summers never tanned.

"Why, God? Why did I agree?" The words tumbled out helplessly.

A-gree, a-gree, mocked the churning wheels that were carrying her from Cedar Ridge, a small logging town in northwest Washington State, forty miles west to Bellingham, her new home. Home? Never! When she finished school she would go back to Mama and Dad, her brothers, sisters, and friends.

Trinity resolutely lifted her chin. No one had forced her to start school when she was five. No one had forced her to follow dear Mr. Conroy's suggestion that she take the eighth grade state exams when she finished seventh grade. She had wanted to do it then, never thinking of the inevitable result, never thinking that Cedar Ridge had no accredited school beyond the eighth grade.

If she had known how Mr. Conroy's coaching over the next two years would prepare her so well the tests

administered by the high school in Bellingham seemed
easy, would she have done her best?

Her chin wavered. God had given her intelligence and
expected her to use it, her parents always said.

"Two years," she whispered, shuddering. "I should
feel proud. How many not-yet fifteen year olds enter
their junior year? Besides, I'll be staying with Grandma
Clarissa's friends. The Butterfields' letter said all I had
to do was wipe the dishes at night and watch the two
little ones when they go out in the evenings." Tears
welled in her eyes. No small Butterfields could take the
place of baby Albert at home who had howled when she
left. Ed and Vi, just younger than Trinity, had looked as
if they wanted to join in. Hope and Faith, her older
sisters, had looked solemn in their Sunday best. Hope
whispered, "Remember, you'll be home at Christmas."

Four months. *Could a ball of misery live that long?*
Trinity wondered.

The sudden memory of her over-six-foot tall father
towering above her five-foot three-inch mother Mercy
quieted the distraught girl. "You can do what you must,"
Edmund Mason softly said. "And you must finish school
and become what God intends you to be."

Trinity sighed and wadded her lace-edged handkerchief into a crumpled knot. Only too well did she know
how set her parents were on their children getting an
education. A dear cousin with no job training had been
widowed and left with several children and another on
the way. She was finally offered a job cooking for the
wheat harvesters while a sister watched her children.
Seeing her struggles had made Mercy and Edmund
determined none of their children would have to suffer

for lack of a marketable skill.

Trinity mentally turned her back on the past. If only the future weren't so frightening! What if the Bellingham girls laughed at her, or worse, at the clothes Mama had carefully fitted, copying the latest magazine styles? She smoothed a wrinkle from her long, dark blue skirt and straightened her plain white shirtwaist. With her frogged dark blue coat Mama had stitched so carefully she felt like a wren beside peacocks next to the elaborate dresses and coats and beflowered hats of the other passengers. At least her buttoned shoes were new.

A new horror attacked the sensitive girl. Would God punish her if she changed her name to Elizabeth or Sarah or anything but Trinity? Until now she'd laughed with the rest of the family about how she got her name. When she was born, her oldest sister overheard her parents talking about names. She pointed to herself—"Faith." She pointed to her younger sister.—"Hope." Then she pointed to the new baby, but her face puckered with thought. Suddenly she jumped up and down. A smile lit her face—"Trinity!"

"Even if she's a little mixed up, it shows she's been listening to your sermons," Mercy teased Edmund. "Trinity our little one will be."

It hadn't mattered in Cedar Ridge, but it did now. Trinity pressed her hot forehead against the cool window. They had left the dark forests with glimpses of snow-capped Mount Baker and shining silver streams. Open valleys lay ahead, with a few farms now and then nestled into wooded hillsides. A large body of water Trinity knew to be Bellingham Bay sparkled in the distance. With a mournful whistle of farewell to all she held dear, the train slowed, chugged past several buildings, and came to a stop.

Trinity gathered her scant possessions, took a deep breath that made her heart ache even more, and stepped into an unfamiliar world, her only security the love of her Heavenly Father and her faith in His Son.

one
Early Summer 1918

She didn't look back. She didn't dare.

Only after the eastbound train hurled around a bend and gathered enough momentum that a leap to freedom would mean certain death did twenty-year-old Trinity Mason unclench her fingers and stare out the window Her future seemed bleak indeed.

Ba-ack, ba-ack, taunted the clacking wheels. Trinity's blue eyes darkened to almost black, matching the soft waves that framed her ivory cheeks and were gathered into a loose knot at the nape of her neck. "Why, God? Is there no other way?"

No-way, no-way, mocked the churning wheels carrying her from Bellingham to Cedar Ridge, almost six years after that fateful September day in 1912. A bitter smile marred Trinity's features. How could she ever have cried herself to sleep those long-ago first nights in Bellingham?

Bellingham, that beautiful city by Bellingham Bay, was the home of Bellingham Normal School where she had spent two happy years after high school graduation training to be a teacher. Soon she would be issued a Life Certificate that guaranteed her the right to teach anywhere in the state of Washington.

Trinity sighed. How distant were those days when she lived waiting for her first Christmas vacation at home! In the hard studying that followed, the making of friends at school, and in the little church where the pastor preached the Gospel as her own father did, the homesick girl gradually grew away from Cedar Ridge. *Never from the family*, she quickly thought. Deep loyalties provided a little comfort now that she had been called back into exile. The interurban rides, moonlight beach picnics, Bible study groups, and church activities would now have to become only memories.

Why must Germany wish to conquer the world? A few short years ago the devastating panorama about to unfold on the world would have seemed unthinkable. Indeed the 1914 assassination of Archduke Ferdinand had triggered a bizarre chain of events that brought Trinity Mason to a crossroads in her life.

The past continued to haunt her. Did the young Trinity still exist, hidden deep inside beneath the dark skirt and spotless white middy blouse that faintly resembled her going-away outfit years ago? If not, why was she here?

The plush seats and brass kerosene lamps hanging from the ceiling and around her faded and a multitude of scenes filled her vision. Mama's letter just a few months earlier asking her to come home was still fresh in her mind.

> *We need you . . . Ed has already enlisted now that America has gone to war. He's at Camp Lewis. Faith is run ragged teaching at the Prairie School. The school is too far out of town for her to live at home and help with the war efforts.*
>
> *While we rejoice over Hope's great opportunity to continue to teach in the Panama Canal Zone, we cannot rely on her help. Besides, her place is with her husband. We're just thankful she met such*

*a wonderful man on her way down last year. We
believe it is more than chance that he took the
same ship on his way back to his police job there
that carried our Hope.*

*This leaves you, Trinity. Vi is a great help and
even little Albert at ten just about runs his legs off.
We'd never remind you of your promise except in
the direst circumstances. But with a new baby on
its way at my age and due in December and your
father not at all well, there seems to be no choice.*

*Grandma Clarissa hasn't been too well either
since Grandpa died and she came to live with us.
I know you've made a wonderful record and we're
proud of you. Trinity, please come home for the
summer. See if the school board will release you
midterm so you can be here after the baby comes.*

Your loving Mother.

Concern over her family drove some of the resentment from Trinity's heart. Mama was old to be having
another baby and at Christmastime Dad hadn't looked
well. He carried the sorrows of the community as all
good shepherds did. Having her home could lift some of
the burdens—but what about her?

"God, am I just being selfish?" she whispered so low
not even the man in front of her could hear. "I should be
glad, glad, glad to help my family but oh, how I'll miss
Bellingham."

Her mind flew to the tiny but immaculate rooms she
rented that now lay empty, bare of everything that had
made them hers. The Butterfields had added on a little
sitting room for her when she finished Normal School

and decided to remain with them. It gave her privacy and a place to read, correct papers, and dream. Of course when would-be beaux called, she met them only in the formal downstairs parlor with its horsehair furniture and red plush drapes, worn but still faintly elegant.

What would John think when he received her letter? Her heart fluttered with a strange kind of relief. John Standish, with hair as fair as the blowing wheat on his enormous ranch in Canada, had sought an introduction to Trinity after first seeing her in the Bellingham Bank. Unlike the boys who followed her and vied for the privilege of escorting her from church by bashfully saying, "I'm going your way," John scorned such subterfuge.

"Miss Mason," he said immediately after being introduced one Sunday evening following church, "I have my automobile here and will be happy to take you and your friends home." Letty and Mollie almost melted on the spot but Trinity simply thanked him, gathered her soft white skirt around her, and stepped into the front seat when he held the door open.

John managed effectively to block other beaux until Trinity knew he had begun to care for her.

One part of her remained flattered and thrilled that such a "good catch" singled her out. But Trinity also saw how John's feelings could not be laughed off the way she had fended away any hint of sentimentality from others.

At least her departure would allow time to think. She knew no amount of wealth would tempt her unless she also learned to love John with all her heart. What would he do? Follow her? A delicious chill left her shaken.

How would Cedar Ridge appear to someone with his background? Would he meet the inevitable test of Dad's keen searching if things grew serious?

Trinity impatiently shoved aside such musings. She had enough to consider without worrying over something that might never happen.

The little train had slowed to wind up a steep hill. Its *chug-chug-chug* reminded Trinity of the many times she had sat in this same car coming and going between two different worlds. City and hamlet. Mountains and shore. Years as well as miles apart in customs, ideas, and opportunities. "I feel like a wishbone," Trinity admitted. "Pulled and pulled. Will I break?" She thought of the jagged splinters left when a wishbone gave way and chided herself for self-pity. *The Lord loves a cheerful giver*, she reminded herself, and quickly added in her heart, *but You're going to have to give me the strength to be one*.

Thankfulness for her wellspring of strength filled her. Time after time God had provided when she needed power beyond her own to meet situations. A trill of laughter escaped into the quiet car. How could she forget her Father's help the day of her student teaching demonstration?

Only fervent prayer that day had prevented her undoing. The day the supervisors filed into the back of the room to observe her fell on the day she had scheduled the teaching of the letter **F**. What should she do? She had no time to prepare other lesson plans. Bolstered by her Scottish-Irish stubbornness, she raised her chin, gave thanks her long skirt hid her shaking knees, and began.

"Today we're going to learn the letter **F**. I want each

of you to repeat after me. **F**." A chorus of **F**s from the row of solemn professors sent through her an insane desire to laugh. She bit her lip.

"Now, Johnny." She addressed the most serious of her observers and pretended he was a five year old. "A big dog chased a cat up a tree. When the cat reached safety on a limb, it looked down at the dog. What did it say?"

"*Ffffff*," the good professor replied.

"Right. And that's the sound **F** makes." Trinity went on with the lesson but unashamedly eavesdropped when the bell released her. Gratitude to God filled her when she overheard the professor she had nicknamed Johnny chuckle and say, "I like that young woman's approach. It's fresh and children are bound to respond to it, and to her. When she's ready, we'll find her a good school."

The professor proved as good as his word. He wrote up a report of her demonstration in such glowing terms Trinity was offered a job teaching third grade in an outlying Bellingham school, one close enough to town that she could ride the interurban and remain with the Butterfields.

"It's a fairy tale," she exulted when she got final word of her acceptance. "Can you believe it? A whole sixty-five dollars every month! I'll take out just what I need and send the rest home. They can certainly use it." A cloud crossed her bright future. "They've sacrificed so much for me to get through school now I can begin to repay them."

For two years—from 1916 to 1918—Trinity taught and won the hearts of her students and their parents. Her eyes shone when her principal called her in at the end of the year and told her because she had shown excellence in service she would receive seventy dollars a month for the next year. With America still at war she rejoiced. Every bit of money helped.

Then Mama's letter came, and Trinity's dreams of spending the summer taking further schooling were dismissed. Before Trinity stopped reeling with disappointment, however, a bolt to rival lightning split her world even wider.

She hummed to herself one late May afternoon in an attempt to banish fear about Ed, the war, and the coming summer at home. The war had surely brought an influx of new songs. Sheet music appeared regularly on the Butterfields' piano, a hint for Trinity and their friends to feel welcome and sing. She knew the strains of "Roses in Picardy," and "Long, Long Trail" brought thoughts to her hosts of their son now fighting overseas.

"We've put our boy in the Lord's keeping," round-faced Mrs. Butterfield once said, her hands busy with a shapeless mass of dough destined to become the lightest of rolls. One tear fell and she wiped it away, leaving a flour streak on her cheek. "Now He knows what's best and I guess He doesn't want us moping." Her hands stilled. "Time enough for sadness if . . . ."

Trinity never forgot the moment and the good woman's faith added another pearl to the girl's string of experiences that brightened the hardest, darkest days.

"Trinity? Someone here to see you," Mrs. Butterfield called up the stairs. Trinity finished patting her dark waves into place and skipped down. Probably John. She hoped he wasn't going to declare himself.

A tall, heavy-set man, the antithesis of John, awaited her. "Miss Trinity, do you remember me?"

"Why—" She searched her memory. "Of course. You're Joe Baldwin. What are you doing here in the big city?"

With the usual Cedar Ridge directness, Joe Baldwin looked straight into her surprised blue eyes. "To get you."

"*What*?" Fear zigzagged through her body. Her mouth went dry. "Mama, Dad—is everyone all right?"

"Fine, just fine." His hearty tone left no room for doubt.

"Then, why—?"

"Miss Trinity," Joe began, twirling his big hat in gnarled hands, "the way I hear it, you're about the best teacher in western Washington."

Red flags few in her white cheeks.

"Now, we're building a new one-room school just five miles out of Cedar Ridge. We need the best teacher we can find—and from where I stand, that's you." His gaze never left hers.

"I talked with the head men up at the Normal School. Didn't want to just go on Cedar Ridge hearsay." A grin lightened his weathered face. "When I told them what I had in mind, why, they said they wouldn't stand in your way."

"I'm not sure I understand," Trinity faltered. "A one-room school? I teach third grade."

He dismissed her weak protest. "According to those who know best, you're qualified to teach all eight grades."

"Yes, but—"

"How much are you making a month, if you don't mind saying?"

"It will be seventy dollars next term." Her brain whirled. Did God have anything to do with Mr. Baldwin's offer?

"I'll give you double, 140 dollars a month, if you take the job," Joe stated flatly.

The floor felt strange beneath her feet. She gasped at the unbelievable sum. It would take her years and years to ever build up to such a magnificent salary, even if she earned a raise every single year.

"Mr. Baldwin, I think we'd better sit down." With a silent prayer for guidance, Trinity seated herself and waited until the courteous logger did the same. "Is—is there some catch? Something I need to know about this job?"

He laid his hat on the floor and his frank gaze met hers. "The fact is, we've had a mite of trouble with some of the bigger boys who should be in eighth grade. They've been going to another school an' the teacher let them get the upper hand. Don't worry, Miss Trinity. We've told them this is their last chance. One crack out of the bucket and they're out—for good." He smiled and she relaxed a bit.

"Now, my wife and me will be proud to have you board with us durin' the week and we'll see to it you get home for the weekends, too, any time you want to go. We figure what you eat won't cost much, so if you want to give my missus twenty dollars a month we'll call it square."

Trinity felt her jaw drop. Even the Butterfields charged thirty-five dollars a month and that was rock bottom for board and room. Still she hesitated. "I've already said I'd come back here next year."

"Sho', that's no problem." Joe clapped his hat on and stood. "The Cedarton school building won't be ready until after Christmas. The school board here's so glad you can earn more than what they pay, why, they said if you'll just teach 'til Christmas they'll release you. Is it a deal?" He hesitated, then a warm, slow smile crossed his face. "Don't answer now. I've got an old friend here I've been hankerin' to look up. Why don't you take tonight to think about it? I guess it's kinda a shock, an' all. I'll be back tomorrow."

"Good afternoon, Mr. Baldwin." Trinity held out one trembling hand, still dazed by the rapid succession of events.

"Better make that Joe, Miss Trinity. I allow how you'll be livin' with us." He squeezed her hand until she wanted to yell, bowed, and whistled his way out and down the steps.

What should she do? she thought wildly.

All evening Trinity paced the floor, glad for the Butterfields' absence. The quiet house reached out to her, reminding her of the happy years once she had overcome her early homesickness and learned to love the Butterfields.

Yet how could she refuse this opportunity? The much-needed money could make a crucial difference. So could her presence at home on the weekends. If she did the heavy cleaning, baking, and laundry then, Vi and Albert could manage during the week. Was it right to even think of refusing because the prospect of going back appalled her?

For hours she battled, determined to be objective, yet knowing every tick of the clock brought her closer to the end of her Bellingham era. At last she dropped to her knees and poured out her heart in prayer.

"Oh, Lord, you know me. You know my fears and desires and rebelliousness. I don't want to go back, to try and teach all eight grades in a crowded little school! I want to stay here, to be someone. Please, what shall I do?"

Breathless, hoping for an answer, she waited.

Nothing happened.

She prayed again, more fervently, until she could honestly say, "Not my will, but Thine." Exhausted, and still unclear as to the answer, she rose and prepared for bed. By the time the Butterfields returned that night, no crack of light showed under her doorway. She heard their quiet movements and then silence.

Outside her open window the friendly moon shone anxiously on the troubled young woman. The fragrance of climber roses on the tall trellis just outside spilled into her room. A seagull mourned in the distance.

"Lord, in James 1:5 we're told that if we lack wisdom to ask You and it shall be given. You've directed my paths all of my life. If I ever needed Your guidance, it's now."

Scarcely had the words slipped from her mouth than the room seemed to change to her home just after Trinity's high school graduation. She could see in detail Dad, Mama, and Grandma Clarissa who moved in after Grandpa died, and Faith, Hope, and herself in light muslin dresses. Work caught up for a change, they rested in rockers and chairs and the wide front porch swing. Trinity loved such rare occasions with Vi and Ed off at their own games and baby Albert asleep in his corner of the porch after assuring them he was "too ol' to have a nap."

"I'm glad the children are playing," Grandma began. "I have something to say to you older ones."

Trinity glanced up from the embroidered pillowcase she had almost finished for her hope chest. Faith and Hope did the same. The family resemblance of wholesome attractiveness gave the scene a quiet charm.

"You insisted that I live with you and I am glad." Tiny Grandma, with her wise eyes and wide lap that encouraged children's confidences! "Now I can return something."

A chorus of protest rose. "*Return*? Goodness, Grandma, you're never still. Who mends the piles of stockings and makes cookies when Mama's too busy?"

She laughed and the familiar crinkles creased her faded roseleaf cheeks. A little color touched them and she pulled a letter from inside the little shawl she wore even on warm days.

"What's that, Grandma?" Trinity forgot to be polite.

"It's a torch."

"A *what*?" Hope's mouth dropped open and Trinity craned her neck to get a better look. What could Grandma mean by that?

"Girls, mind your manners," their mother said.

"Yes, Mama." They subsided, but Trinity couldn't keep her gaze off the letter with spidery writing Grandma took from the envelope.

"It really is a torch," Grandma insisted. A small smile played around her lips. "Remember your father's sermon last week? *'Thy word is a lamp unto my feet, and a light unto my path.'* Psalm 119:105." She smiled at their growing puzzlement then turned serious.

"Girls, you're at a time where you must choose your lives. None of you is old enough to marry except Faith and she hasn't found the right person yet. You know that as far back as we can trace, our ancestors were God-fearing, upright men and women. Our families on both sides have held high the lamp of God's Word, often in terrible darkness. From the time they left Scotland and Ireland years ago and came to America, they have been among the settlers, pioneers, and brave-hearted ones who overcame evil with their lamp in darkness."

In the little pool of silence Trinity thought how in the late 1800s Grandma and Grandpa Mason came to Cedar Ridge, bringing their sturdy Scottish-Irish bodies and minds and hearts to the dark forest. They helped establish the first school, arranged for the first church to be built, and rejoiced when their son Edmund became a minister and returned to Cedar Ridge. If ever the lamp of God's Word had been needed, it was in that rough and tumble outpost that once saw murderous fights every Saturday night and injured men who required the doctor's services by lamplight.

"What does this have to do with us, Grandma?" Trinity asked in spite of her mother's frown and slight shake of head.

Veined hands smoothed the letter in Clarissa's lap. "Every generation must eventually pass the torch to the next. Grandpa's gone now and I'm getting old." She raised her hand to still the girls' involuntary protest. "I plan to be with you for a long time but my feet and hands are slowing." She looked at each of the girls in turn: Faith, so strong and patient; Hope, fiery with life; and

Trinity, teetering behind childhood and womanhood.

"A distant cousin I barely knew has left me a small inheritance. Not a lot but enough to give you each a chance for Normal School, if you want to go."

Normal School! Trinity pinched herself. She and her sisters had already discussed attending the two-year college course at Bellingham Normal School that would result in a Life Diploma to teach anywhere in the state of Washington. With Ed and Vi and Albert needing schooling, the older girls had resigned themselves to seeking some honorable work to help out.

"Wouldn't it be better to give it to Mama and Dad for the children?" Unselfish Faith's suggestion sent a pang of disappointment through Trinity. She'd already envisioned herself swishing into her own school and teaching small children.

"No, my dear. We will get by on what we earn. This windfall must go to the work of the Lord and I can think of nothing better than investing in your futures so you can teach little children."

Trinity's spirits leaped. "Really, Grandma?" She left her chair and knelt at her grandmother's knees.

"There is just one thing," said Clarissa hesitating, her face troubled. Faith and Hope knelt beside Trinity. "When you accept the help I can give, it is with the understanding you must pass it on. That means when it's time for Ed and Vi and even Albert to need support, you girls must be responsible. If the time ever comes and I or your parents call on you to sacrifice for the sake of the others, you must do it." Her keen eyes searched their faces.

"Of course." Faith sounded choked up and she blinked

hard.

Hope raised her shoulders in an almost imperceptible shrug and agreed. "Yes, Grandma."

"Trinity?"

Why should a little chill touch her, as if the sun had momentarily hidden behind a cloud? Trinity shook her head impatiently and said, "You know we always do what you ask us to." Her wave included her parents.

"Then it's settled." Grandma gently stroked the girls' hair. Trinity felt blessed when Clarissa added, "Never let the torch go out, girls. It may flicker and get low but God's Holy Spirit will renew you and give you the strength and courage to go on."

The scene faded. Trinity drew in a quivering breath. "Thank You, Father." Tomorrow she would say yes to Joe Baldwin—and only God would know how much that one word cost.

two

Crouching shadows sprang to life with the last rays of twilight. An owl hooted in a tall pine that pointed the way to heaven with its ramrod-straight spire. The midsummer moon cautiously raised over a hill, surveyed the valley below, and rose in splendor. It searched for an object worthy of illumination and chose a lone figure silhouetted against the night sky.

The lithe, broad-shouldered young man stood statuelike on the crest of the hill. A curious trick of light and shadow hollowed his face and gave an appearance of added years. Even when Will Thatcher threw his head back and let the light pour over him the illusion remained.

Reassured by the stillness, forest creatures came out. A giant hawk sailed by, searching for food. Rabbits quickly hopped from bright-as-day clearings to the cover of darkness. A porcupine chuckled by, unafraid. The barking of coyotes in the distance enlivened the night.

But Will Thatcher, who had just celebrated his twenty-first birthday, saw or heard little of the beloved symphony. A long night lay ahead, a night of fighting a thousand tempting demons. What better place to contemplate than here where snowcapped Mount Baker dwarfed even the knottiest human problems and stood firm in a world whose very foundations had crumbled?

Protest rose in Will's soul. Must he again sacrifice every dream and every secret desire? Cold sweat filmed his intense blue eyes in spite of the warmth of the night. Bitterness gnawed at his heart. What good had that other sacrifice been—the noble shelving of his future for the sake of others—if he must die on foreign soil? Will's sensitive, curved lips tightened: He would do what he must if called. Until then an eternal round of chores would fill every waking minute.

"What if I had refused?" he challenged the inky blue and silver sky. Only the *whoo, whoo* of a tiny breeze replied. Will flung himself down on a mossy knoll and propped his hands beneath his head. Closing his eyes, in his mind he relived the fateful day five years ago, just days before his sixteenth birthday . . . .

"Will, I need your help," stalwart Lewis Thatcher announced one sunny morning. He stood from the breakfast table and stretched. "Meet me outside when you're through." He strode away without another word.

Caught by an unusual tone in his father's voice, Will quickly finished the biscuit and ham gravy on his plate, decided not to take time for another helping, and wiped his mouth. Moments later he joined Lewis on the front porch of their old-fashioned white frame home in Hamilton, Washington. "What do you need me for?"

Lewis didn't speak for a long time. When he did, the blue eyes that matched his son's held a mixture of excitement and defeat. "I have a chance to buy eighty acres north of here." A sparkle crept into his face. "It's in a valley so rich we'll grow crops enough to feed all of us and make a profit selling to others."

"But Pa, you're a carpenter!" Will could scarcely believe his ears. He ran his fingers through light brown hair that lay in waves deep enough to be the envy of any girl. "That's why we came out from North Carolina. So you could carpenter."

"I know." Lewis Thatcher's features on his "pioneer face"—as his family called it—became more pronounced. "Times got so hard back home my brother Mark and I and a lot of other Tarheels couldn't make a decent living. Washington offered the chance for a new start. Well, I've made it. Now I've saved up enough for a down payment on land about five miles out of Cedar Ridge."

"You've already decided," Will said, wondering what it meant to his own future. A horrifying thought brought him out of his lounging position. "There won't be a high school there, will there? How can I finish my last two years?"

"You won't," he told his son quietly. "Much of the eighty acres is timbered. We'll need to clear before we can plow and plant. We can use the logs to build a new and bigger house, barns, and corral. You've always wanted a horse. Now there will be a place for one."

Will lost track of the conversation after the crushing acknowledgment of the sacrifice he faced. "You mean—"

"It's our chance to make a good life for the family," Lewis pointed out. "I won't be able to do it alone."

"And I'm the oldest."

"Yes." Shame crept into Lewis's honest blue eyes. "I know what I'm asking, Will. I've thought and prayed and tried to come up with another way. I can't. Daniel and Curtis can help some but neither has yet gained a man's strength. Besides, they need more schooling." Pride warred with the natural reticence Pa had toward his children. "I can depend on you to do a man's work. You've made the most of your ten years of school and studied hard."

"If I help for a year or so, can I be spared? I *have* to get an education," Will pleaded. Should he tell Pa how the sight of every bridge, every steel and concrete structure thrilled him? How someday he would be an engineer, responsible for planning and overseeing great buildings? He longed to share his dreams but the sense of duty instilled since childhood stopped him.

Take care of your little brothers. See they don't get into trouble. Don't let anyone pick on Ellen and Rachel and little Andrew. Be a little man, Will. You're Pa's helper. Admonitions rose and bound him with invisible chains.

He jerked his thoughts back to the present when he heard Pa's voice.

"I don't know. Everything will depend on how the crops do and on how much we can put aside. If things go well, perhaps in a year or two something can be worked out. By then Daniel and Curtis will be of more help." Pa suddenly stuck out his hand. "Are you with me, Will?"

"Yes, Pa." His firm young grip tightened but Will ducked his head to hide the rush of regret already attacking him.

All during the selling of the house in Hamilton and the flurry of moving Will stubbornly clung to his dreams. Someday it would be his turn. Someday he would turn over his position to Daniel and be free to pursue his own career. Even if Pa couldn't help, Will would work his way through college and be someone, someday.

His first chance for real independence came when Pa took him to one side the week before they moved to the Cedar Ridge spread. "Think you can drive Old Bossy and our six new cows up by yourself or do you need help?" Pa frowned. "If you can do it, I need Daniel and Curtis with me." He sighed. "I wish I could have managed a horse but that will have to come later. It's a good twenty-five miles. Can you do it?"

Will felt his measure was being taken. He drew himself up to his full six feet and nodded. "Just a nice little stroll, Pa." His twinkly blue eyes matched the sparkle in his father's gaze.

"Twenty-five miles of bawling cows won't be a picnic," Lewis warned but relief showed in his joshing.

"I don't expect it to be." Will set his jaw in the way he had learned since his future changed so drastically.

"There are a few cabins and small places along the way. Any of them will be glad to take you in," Pa advised. "Walk slow but don't loiter, even when you get close to Cedar Ridge and start fording the pretty little trout streams. Time enough for fishing later." A smile softened his stern features.

If Will lived to be older than Methuselah, he'd never forget his first experience herding cows. Old Bossy behaved. The six new cows did not. As Will told Pa later, "What with chasing those critters, I bet I walked closer to fifty miles than twenty-five!" When he finally drove his charges into a rudely constructed corral thrown up to house the cows until Uncle Mark and neighboring men came for a barn-raising, Will didn't care if he ever saw another cow again . . . except sizzling on a steak platter in front of him.

Weeks flew into months. Season followed season. Determined to be ready when his time came, Will spent what little free time he had with his nose in a book. Before leaving Hamilton the persistent young man had arranged with his favorite high school teacher to send him mathematics, literature, history, *and* geography books. The kindly teacher parted with this admonition:

"Remember, some of our country's greatest—including Abraham Lincoln—were self-educated men. Lack of formal schooling is no excuse for ignorance."

So Will muttered equations while he plowed and quoted famous authors while he milked. At the end of the first year Pa said, "If things continue as they have, next year we'll talk about sparing you."

That hope sustained Will when his younger brothers and sisters set off for school in their second Cedar Ridge year. But a long and costly illness that almost took little Andrew followed by a skimpy crop the next year shattered Will's expectations. Instead of freedom to study and forge ahead, spring 1915 found seventeen-year-old Will working in the woods to bring in badly needed cash for the family. The whine of saws, the ring of axes, and the ever-threatening cry of "Timberrrr!" when a forest monarch toppled slowly drowned out his belief life held more for him than loyalty to his family.

Pa never mentioned his eldest son's sacrifice. Yet now and then when Will unexpectedly raised his head, he read in Lewis's blue eyes a poignant appreciation and an apology. His bitterness was held in check until spring 1918 when America entered World War I.

Will Thatcher shifted position, noting how low the moon had fallen. Blanking out his mind he watched it set and in the dark hour preceding dawn he faced Gethsemane and knew a little of what Jesus experienced centuries before. *Had God forsaken Will?*

Never before had Will felt so entirely alone, so cut off

from other human beings. Did each man at some time in his life come to this aloneness? Behind lay disappointment; ahead lay duty, perhaps death. A terrifying moment, this facing of self and God.

With a low cry Will sprang to his feet. Straight from the heart in a voice that began as a whisper and rose to a shout, Will challenged the forces of evil, war, and weakness with the words of poet James Russell Lowell:

> Once to every man and nation comes the moment to decide;
> In the strife of Truth with Falsehood, for the good or evil side;
> Some great cause, God's new Messiah, offering each the bloom or blight;
> Parts the goats upon the left hand and the sheep upon the right,
> And the choice goes by forever 'twixt that darkness and that light.

Exaltation filled him. He mentally reviewed more verses, discarded them, then filled with the Holy Spirit his strong voice rang out in affirmation.

> By the light of burning heretics Christ's bleeding feet I track,
> Toiling up new Calvaries ever with the cross that turns not back,
> And these mounts of anguish number how each generation learned
> One new word of that grand *Credo* which in prophet-hearts has burned

Since the first man stood God-conquered with
his face to heaven upturned.*

For the first time since that day of decision Will felt
free. "God-conquered with my face to heaven upturned,"
he paraphrased. His head thrown back and his face wet
with tears, Will knew nothing on earth mattered except
his commitment to whatever cross God gave him.

Hours later Will met Pa at the barn. He had done the
morning milking, cleaned out the stalls, and fed and
watered the animals.

Lewis gazed into his son's face and recoiled. "Son,
where have you been?"

"To the mountaintop." Keen understanding flashed
between them.

"You will never be the same." Lewis swallowed hard.

"No." Will bent to pick up the brimming milk pails.

"William."

Pa's voice stopped him. Only in moments of deepest
stress did Pa use his son's full name. "Yes?"

"After the mountaintop comes the valley." A shroud
of sadness underscored the warning.

"I know, Pa." Will listened to a rooster crow and faced
the morning light that flooded through the barn windows. "Last night—this morning—I know it's to prepare me for something."

"You are a son to be proud of." Lewis made no effort
to hide the sparkling dew in his eyes, but before Will
could answer he added, "Better get the milk in the house.
Your ride to the woods comes early."

---

*From "The Present Crisis" by James Russell Lowell (1819–1891).

Will watched his father march out the open barn door and across to the house. Strange, the shoulders so often bowed with care these days sat square and sturdy and Pa looked as if he kept time to martial music even in his worn barn boots.

For the next few weeks Will held and treasured his mountaintop experience against all adversity, even when his younger brothers and sisters talked about the upcoming school year. But when Daniel insisted he'd had enough learning and had been given a logging job with the same company that employed Will, Will's reverie ended.

"Don't be foolish and throw away your chances," Will ordered. "Don't you want to be someone?"

"I reckon Pa's the best someone I ever knew and he's a logger-farmer," good-natured Daniel retorted. The few freckles on his sunburned elfin nose looked like copper specks. " 'Sides, if I can bring in money maybe you can go be whatever you want to be."

Hope flared inside Will then died. "I'll get called into the army before then, I imagine."

"I may, too," Daniel admitted. "But until I do there's no sense going on to school when all I want to do is work."

Despite Will's raging, his formerly tractable brother dug in his heels and absolutely refused to listen. Even his first few days in the woods that left him exhausted did not discourage him. Gradually Will came to enjoy having Daniel beside him. Always a loner, he found himself accepting Daniel as an equal instead of a younger brother. Most dinner breaks found them a little apart from their fellow loggers sharing in a way they never had been able to before. One day Will opened up and told Daniel of the midsummer night when he faced his God.

Daniel listened quietly, but the look in his eyes was far from placid. "I'm glad you told me. I've always wondered how much stock you took in what Pa and Ma taught us about God."

Will caught a yearning wistfulness and instantly replied, "I know now life isn't worth living without that faith."

"Then it's all right," said Daniel smiling. "I decided that when I knew we might get called to fight." He idly picked at a blade of grass. "News is the war might be over soon. I hope so. Not that I'm afraid to go. It's just that so far I haven't really given much to the world. I'd like to make some kind of mark before my number comes up." He leaped to his feet. "Better get back to work."

Their talk sank deep into Will's consciousness. How well he knew the futile longing to make a mark! Would he? With his new commitment to God and His Son somehow it seemed more possible than a few weeks earlier. He whistled while he sawed and chopped and managed to recapture some of that life-changing experience, sharing deeply with Daniel whenever they had time.

From mountaintop to valley, as Pa said, came without warning. A half-hour before quitting time on a drizzly late-September afternoon Will and Daniel finished sawing through an enormous fir tree. They'd made their undercut on the other side and gauged the path of the tree's fall. In a bizarre twist, when the fir fell it changed direction, straight toward a widowmaker.*

"*Run!*" Will screamed, and he tore toward Daniel who

---

*A dead tree, a snag.

stood directly in the big tree's path.

Daniel leaped for safety, but it was too late.

The falling tree continued its ponderous drop, tearing limbs from other trees as it crashed to the ground. To Will's utter horror Daniel fell. A heartbeat later the tree toppled onto his prone body.

Will screamed for help and then with superhuman strength attacked the enemy tree with his bare hands. Arriving loggers pulled him off and chopped as rapidly as they could. Daniel's inert form lay covered with bright stains when they finally freed him.

"Oh, God, no!" Will lifted his brother's broken body and cradled it in his arms. "Daniel, Daniel."

The loggers bared their heads and stood silent, too wise to hope in the face of the evidence before them. A ragged gasp ran through the circle of rough, caring men when Daniel opened pain-dazed eyes.

"Will?"

"I'm here." Tears splashed on the twisted face.

"I'm—glad. Tell Pa, and Ma—guess I won't make mark—" His eyes cleared and he looked beyond Will, up, past the waving treetops. A glorious smile erased the pain in his face and brightened it until his freckles shone. "It doesn't matter—now."

Daniel's eyes closed but the light stayed in his face even when he went slack in Will's arms. The others slowly withdrew, leaving a heartbroken man holding the brother he had learned to love more than life itself.

After a long time he stood. It was long past time to go home.

three

Will felt propelled by a silent screaming inside all the way down the steep mountainside to the jitney* that carried the logging crew to and from the woods.

Take care of your little brothers. See they don't get into trouble.

Only when his arms threatened to give out did he surrender his place among the four men carrying the stretcher bearing Daniel's body. How he made it remained dim in his mind forever. The awful feeling he should have been able to save Daniel joined with dread. *What would Pa and Ma do? Oh, dear God, if this were only a nightmare from which he could awaken!*

Much later Will roused to the touch of his head logger's rough hand on his shoulder.

"Better go prepare the folks, son." Kindness showed in every seam of the weathered face.

Will staggered out of the jitney. *Too late!* Pa and Ma must have seen the jitney pull to the side of the dusty road and stop instead of merely halting to let off Will and Daniel. They ran down the lane leading from the big log house the Thatchers had built the first summer after they reached Cedar Ridge. Young Curtis, Ellen, Rachel, and even Andrew followed.

"*Will? Daniel?*" Pa managed to gasp between heavy breathing.

Will shook his head. "Pa, he's—"

---

* A buslike vehicle.

35

Ma's glazed eyes staring behind Will whipped him around. Four earth-stained loggers carried a blanket-shrouded figure that told the story.

"Not Daniel! Oh, God, not Daniel!" Ma screamed.

Something in Will snapped. *Why would Ma say such a thing? Did she wish it had been Will instead?* He brokenly tried to reach out to her but Ruth Thatcher had flown to the stretcher and buried her face in the folds of the faded blanket.

"Where were you, Will?" Did he imagine it or had doubt and accusation crept into Pa's eyes? A red-hot poker of pain seared Will's heart and he could only shake his head.

"Not a thing anyone could do," the head logger said soberly. "First thing we knew, Will was yelling for help an' diving toward Daniel." He mopped his sweaty forehead. "It's a miracle you didn't lose two sons instead of one."

"Thank God!" Pa's fervent prayer started Will's heart beating again.

Later Will sought him out for a private moment. "If only he'd listened and stayed in school. Why didn't I make him?" Pa seized his eldest son in a mighty grip and shook him as a cat shakes a mouse. His blue eyes blazed. "William, much as we want to, we can't decide for anyone on this earth except ourselves." Pain laced his denunciation. "You think I don't want to step in and make choices for my family? I do and once—when I asked you to help me—I did."

His face changed. "I've regretted it ever since. At the time I felt we had no choice. But son, it makes no more sense for you to feel this is your fault than for me to believe if we'd stayed in Hamilton this wouldn't have happened." The hands that bit deep into Will's arms loosened. "Looking back does no good." For the first time, Pa looked old and almost beaten.

The next moment he raised his strong head and gazed into the achingly blue sky. "I reckon if I could know Daniel had got right with God and accepted Jesus into his heart—"

"He had, Pa." Some of Will's agony faded. "Just a few days ago we talked." In stumbling words Will told what Daniel said.

Pa's fingers tightened again until sturdy as he was Will wanted to cry out. "Tell Ma, right away. It'll bring what comfort there is." But it wasn't until the sorrowful little family gathered for family worship after a long-delayed evening meal that Will had a chance. When he did, Ma's somber dark eyes didn't lighten but a perceptible relaxing of the muscles in her closed face showed Will Pa had been right.

Out of tragedy came a few rays of light. Will had never felt the love and support of neighbors the way he did now. They came with cooked food. They stopped by and helped with chores. And always they left the warmth of their caring and prayers. Will also drew closer to Pa. That first talk led to others, but one stood out. Will had thought about Pa's admonition on trying to direct others' lives. Encouraged, Pa added more from the deep store of wisdom gained while uprooting and cleaning enormous stumps and following the plow in the straightest furrows to be found.

"Don't you ever wish God would just make folks do what they ought to?" Will asked the morning of Daniel's funeral.

"Amen! It's a good thing I'm not God." Pa's lips set in a grim line. "Sometimes I even go so far as to tell Him so."

"Really, Pa?" Will had never suspected such a thing. "Then what?"

Pa slowly said, "He kind of reminds me in my heart that if God Himself has enough faith in folks not to interfere with their choices—even when He may hate and despise those choices—why, I have to do the same." His farseeing eyes looked across the fields dotted with autumn's orange and gold dying leaves. "It's hard, though."

Will couldn't speak then or later when well-meaning friends offered rude comfort.

"It ain't like he wasn't ready," one good woman said. "Or like he was your Pa and Ma's only boy."

What difference does that make? Will wanted to shout. As he spun on his heels and rushed away, he heard the woman exclaim, "Land sakes, he's taking it hard."

Will walked for hours in the moist fall night. His faith in God remained intact but the need for companionship grew. The loss of Daniel had created a void in himself. Never one to surround himself with comrades, Will preferred his own company or that of a choice few. Daniel had slipped into his life after they began working together and he had provided the missing part.

Gradually life took up its usual pace. Will had little time for solitude except at night and logging and chores left him too tired to appreciate those hours. He had a new logging partner now. Donald McKenna, one of Daniel's best friends, had begged the head logger to let him work with Will and assign whatever new man they hired to

Donald's former partner. The head logger had consented kindly on behalf of Will.

Red-headed Donald didn't attempt to avoid discussing Daniel. Once he said with misty auburn eyes, "If we never talk about him it's like he never lived."

The more Will thought of it, the more sense it made. Ma seldom mentioned Daniel and Will knew the hurt she carried made it worse. He began to pray for her, pleading with God to somehow help them—and Ma— through this.

A few days later he tore into the quiet kitchen. "Ma! Come see the gorgeous rainbow." He raced upstairs. "Ma! Where are you?" His racing feet stilled in the open doorway of his parents' bedroom. "What—"

His question died on his lips. The most beautiful music he had ever heard swelled and shimmered in the quiet room. Ma stood transfixed with one hand on an open bureau drawer. Soft light filtered through hand-made lace curtains and shifted and changed. So did the music. It seemed to come from that open drawer, but how could it? Rising and falling, the notes of liquid clearness like a thrush at prayer crept into Will's heart. He saw Ma's face brighten and her eyes fill for the first time since Daniel's death.

For a minute, an hour, an eternity—Will didn't know which— the birdsong symphony could be heard. Then with a glorious finale it ceased.

Like one awakening from a dream, Ma moved. Her gaze sought Will. "My son, my splendid son!" She tottered toward him and wept in his arms, washing away the last lingering hurt and doubt of her love for him.

"How did it happen?" he asked when they at last sat

down on the bed.

"I had to know he was with God. I had to be sure, in spite of what he told you. I've prayed and prayed. I finally just told God I didn't see how I could go on without some kind of sign." Her eyes filled again. "I know it's probably being weak in the faith but God heard my pitiful cry and had mercy on me." Some of the glory Will had seen in her face returned. "No matter what anyone says, ever, I know my son's with His Son and someday I'll see them both." The last word dropped to a whisper.

Will put his hot face into her aproned lap, something he hadn't done since he was a small child. There had been too many others coming after him who needed that lap for childish hurts. Every trace of guilt that had lingered now vanished.

"I wonder why just you and I heard the music," he finally said.

Ma's hand lay light on the crisp waves of bright brown hair now tousled in her lap. "Perhaps we needed it most. God has comforted Pa and the others in different ways."

Great rejoicing followed the late afternoon experience. Ellen and Rachel wished out loud they could have heard the music, too. "God's ways aren't our ways," Pa said sternly. "He sends what we need when we need it most."

He smiled and added, "Just stay close to our Lord and trust Him. Never envy others' experiences but seek and find your own." Peace seemed to fill the family circle.

A few days later Pa called Will apart from the others. "We're pretty caught up on the chores. Why don't you whistle up Tige and take Saturday off? Maybe you can bring home a deer. I've a hankering for venison steaks."

"Will you come with me?" Will was already planning what he'd need to pack if he left Friday night.

"No, I promised Curtis I'd take him pheasant hunting. He needs some extra rifle practice before I let him out alone." Pa thought for a minute. "Why don't you ask Donald? Or Jimmy Crowfoot? He and his tribe will be here tomorrow to winter in the big meadow back of the south forty."

Will thought of his Indian friend his own age who had been coming every fall for years. "Good idea. He and Donald get along and both are good company."

On Friday night the three lounged around a fire built with an enormous stump as a backlog. October had heralded and brought frosty evenings and the fire felt good. Will finished the last of the cookies Ruth Thatcher sent and grinned, satisfied. "Good thing we're only going to be here one night, the way you two eat."

Indignant, Donald said, "Don't think Jimmy and I didn't notice you ate four helpings of fried potatoes, not counting all the beans and meat and most of those cookies!" Tige, the black Labrador, growled in agreement.

Jimmy just smiled, his dark face expressing wordless enjoyment. Not many white men earned a smile from him but Thatcher's and McKenna's honest dealing and frank friendship had long ago welded bonds of brotherhood. The Thatcher boys and Donald were among the select few with whom Indian loggers would consent to work.

Little by little the bantering changed. Great stars blazed down through sentinel trees and cast an unearthly light on the already frost-covered world. Every blade of grass glistened under its coating of rime.

Will hunkered down farther under his heavy wool blanket. "Well, boys, I guess this will be our last hunting trip for a while."

"How come?" Donald's half-closed eyes opened wide and Jimmy Crowfoot grunted in surprise.

"My papers came today. I'll be reporting to Camp Lewis soon." His long arm reached for a stout stick and stirred the glowing embers into flames, exposing their faces.

"Then I'll enlist and go with you." Donald leaped up, stamped his feet, and blew out a gust of air that quivered in the cold night.

"You'd do that for me?" Will's eyes stung.

Donald shrugged. "Why not? How about it, Jimmy? Want to come? We can be like those three guys in that book—you know, one for all, all for one. Who were they, anyway, Prof?" He turned to Will.

"The Three Musketeers. Dumas wrote it." But Will's gaze switched to Jimmy Crowfoot. Why did Donald blurt out such a thing? Why should Jimmy fight for a country that had mistreated his people so decisively? Will wanted to kick Donald when he continued to prod Jimmy.

"Well?"

Jimmy uncoiled from his position on his tarp. His blanket dropped unheeded to the ground and revealed the lithe, deerskin-clad figure. His coal-black eyes never wavered. "I'll go with you." Before either could speak, Jimmy slipped inexplicably from the firelit circle into the night. He reappeared just before Will and Donald fell asleep, sliding into his blankets and pulling the tarp up around him to keep off the heavy dew that came with morning.

"Don't tell my folks," Will said at breakfast. "I don't want them to know. I'll just leave a note when I have to go so they won't start worrying right away." He quickly changed the subject to the day ahead before either of his comrades could respond.

Alone on a deer trail after having agreed to separate and cover more territory, Will had a chance to reflect. He had spoken truly the night before. This could be his last hunt, his last trip up the timbered slopes past brush thickets he knew and loved. Perhaps a slight melancholy colored his feelings and sharpened his vision but never had the forests and mountains seemed more beautiful. Drifting, swirling leaves of red, orange, gold, and rust contrasted sharply with the white-frosted peaks and bluer-than-sapphire skies. Shades of green offered relief from the blazing vine maples and cottonwoods. He dropped his hand to Tige's sleek back.

Although he knew a single shot would bring Jimmy and Donald, Will felt the same loneliness creep into his heart that had been haunting him ever since he received his marching orders. Faces of friends rose, young men, girls Will knew would gladly accept him as a beau. He shrugged. He'd never yet seen a girl who interested him enough to offer more than friendship. Pa said God had led him to Ma, or her to him. Will grinned, thinking of Pa as a young man in North Carolina teaching school and falling in love with Ruth, one of his pupils!

They'd had a good marriage. Not ones to express their feelings in front of their children, their quiet exchange of glances across the dinner table spoke volumes to Will.

He determined never to marry until he felt what he saw in his folks' eyes.

No danger of his being forgotten while gone, Will thought ruefully. He'd had to dodge some well-set snares from a few of the Cedar Ridge girls who didn't have the sense to know if he wanted them around, *he'd* make the first move. He'd grown adept at simply not being around when those he considered too silly for words stalked him by playing up to Ellen and Rachel.

"The only girl close by that I like to be around is Faith Mason," he told an inquisitive woodpecker who tapped back an answer against a tree trunk. He thought to himself about Faith. She's modest and nice, and she's enough older that I don't have to worry about being chased. He laughed aloud. Faith was doing a fine job teaching the young ones and Will knew his father was going to ask her to live with the Thatchers now that the Browns were moving. She would be good company for Ma and the kids. In fact, Donald had been taking a shine to Faith lately. Will thought they'd make a good pair— if he comes back.

With a thud Will fell from pleasant musing to reality. None of them might come back or, if they did, what shape would they be in? He'd rather die and lie in a lonely, unmarked grave somewhere in France than come home gassed or broken, to be a burden on someone. Uncertainty filled him. Nothing would stop him from going but shouldn't he try and discourage Donald and Jimmy?

A shot. A second. Will bounded to his feet and waited. A faint yell in the distance reached him, then the crashing of brush to his left. He snapped his rifle to his shoulder, threw a shell into the chamber, and waited. Within seconds a buck deer leaped into view. Tige bayed and dashed in pursuit.

Spang.

The buck fell, a beauty. Pa's hankering for venison steaks meant skinning, cutting, and packing out.

"Got him, I see." Donald burst into the small clearing closely followed by Jimmy, whose wide grin bore little resemblance to his usual placid face.

"Jimmy killed his buck, but I shot at this one and missed." Donald looked disgusted. "I was too hurried when I should have taken better aim. When we get to fighting, it will be different."

"Why don't you and Jimmy wait?" Will casually asked. "There's no guarantee we'd be together if you enlist."

Donald scratched his red head. "Jimmy, what do you say? Hey, we'll just wait until you know where you'll be then tell the army if we can't be together, we ain't going."

Jimmy just grinned and took out his hunting knife, hint enough for Will and Donald to attend to the present and let the future alone for now.

For a week Will kept secret the news he had been called up. During that time he visited all his favorite places close to the farm and dropped in on friends to bid an unspoken farewell. Last of all, he returned to the crest of the hill just before dark on his final Saturday night at home.

If the Thatchers hadn't been so busy welcoming Faith Mason into their family circle, he might not have succeeded in his self-imposed silence. As Will returned from the mountain, he was greeted by yellow lamplight spilling from the windows of the log home, merry laughter, and whistles echoing into the night. His dog Tige crouched against his foot and a horse whinnied in the pasture. Only the strength he had received from his tryst with God lent Will enough courage to go inside, pretend all was normal, then excuse himself early and go up to his room.

But before he could throw off the open-necked shirt and jeans, the sound of doors opening and a babble of voices reached him. Will considered climbing into bed the way he was then felt ashamed. His neighbors deserved better. Besides, he heard Ma calling from the foot of the stairs. "Will? Come down, please."

Carefully brushing his hair, he lightly ran downstairs into the living room and looked straight into the most beautiful blue eyes he had ever seen.

four
Autumn 1918

Trinity hurried up the threadbare strip of carpet that graced the center aisle of the little church. Embarrassment and nervousness together sent color to her face. How could she let herself be late to the first fall meeting of the Epworth League,* especially when she had been elected president? All her protests that she'd be leaving after Christmas changed nothing. As long as she remained in Bellingham, her friends wanted her to serve.

In the front row Mollie Perkins fretfully picked at the fine lace trim on her gown and scowled. "I don't see how she does it," she muttered half under her breath into her sister Letty's ear. "*We* dress up and *she* wears a middy and plain gored skirt that barely hides her shabby shoes. Guess who gets all the attention?" Mollie sighed, her gaze glued on the trim girl in navy blue on the raised platform. "I declare, if I didn't love her so much I'd be pea green with envy."

Letty's big brown eyes turned to her pretty blond sister, so unlike her own dark subdued self. "That's it, you know. No one can help loving Trinity, and I'm glad," she added in a burst of honesty. "She has so few clothes, just this outfit and a white one, a couple of wash dresses, and a dark suit and two blouses for teaching, and, oh yes, her mother made her a summer lawn while she was home. Anyway, it's not what she wears, Mollie. It's what she is."

---

*A young people's group.

"I know." Mollie squeezed Letty's hand. "But why didn't *we* think to tuck a late yellow rose in our hair? Maybe then John Standish would look our way. As much as I love Trinity I'd sure beat her time with him if I could!"

"Shhh, we're ready to start," Letty warned. Yet she let her gaze follow Mollie's. Would anyone ever look at her or single her out as John did Trinity? Letty blushed and clasped her hands in her lap, then dared peep across the aisle in the other direction.

From her vantage point in front Trinity saw and correctly interpreted the look. Although her mind was filled with the upcoming meeting, she silently wished Blakely Butterfield, so handsome in his sailor uniform, would see and appreciate Letty's worth . . . instead of sending languishing glances toward the new Epworth League president! Letty would make a faithful, adoring wife to Blakely. While Mollie had more outward beauty, Letty Perkins in her soft blue gown loved the Lord and shyly reflected that love in her brown eyes.

Good heavens, Trinity thought. The last thing I have time for is matchmaking. The idea brought a smile to her lips and she hastily rose. "Let us turn to page 261 and sing 'Day is Dying in the West,' " she announced. The natural blending of many voices sent the lovely words soaring from church windows open to the soft September evening.

Only with a mighty effort could Trinity go on singing. Last spring their songs had held a deeper bass quality; the ranks of young men and boys had thinned since then and Blakely and the few others in uniform could not compensate.

"Pastor Sullivan and I have discussed at length some ideas to help our group grow," Trinity said simply after prayer. "As you know, if ever young people need to know about God's love and His plan of salvation it's now." She raised her chin proudly but her blue eyes darkened. "We all must do everything we can to spread the news of that plan. One way is by increasing attendance at our meetings."

She smiled at their gray-haired, youthful-faced minister. "We propose that our group will be split into two teams. Every Sunday night at our meeting we will tally up points." She ticked them off on her fingers.

"One point is for attendance and an extra point for every new person you bring with you. Another point for each person who memorizes Scripture to quote at the beginning of our service. We'll go right through the alphabet. Next week learn verses that begin with the letter **A**."

She paused and Blakely Butterfield called out, "Too bad we can't start with **J**. We already all know 'Jesus wept.' " Everyone laughed.

Trinity's heart thrilled at the eager agreement in their faces. "Now, once a month Pastor Sullivan will total all the points from the month before. And—" She dramatically lowered her voice, then loudly said, "The team that has the least points must host a social activity for the winners for that month! A party or special event—"

Cheers drowned her out and conversation quieted only when Trinity raised her hand. "Remember, although the socials will be fun, our real purpose is to honor our Lord. We won't give points for those who stay for evening service after our meeting but I hope all of you will make it a regular part of your week."

Her wistful voice and earnest face effectively led into the Bible study two of the boys had prepared, the preselected hymns, and the closing prayer. *And every person stayed*—although a couple of newcomers looked a bit uncomfortable and slid into the back seats. Trinity made a point of following them and making sure they knew the place for the Bible reading and hymns. She felt John's scowl from across the aisle but ignored it. More and more she felt tangled in a web of feelings and his unspoken questions.

She sighed and missed part of the sermon. How long could she keep him from declaring the love she saw in his eyes? Her little ruses to avoid being alone with him had long since worn thin. Why did she feel so mixed up inside? She liked John a great deal. Her heartbeat raced when he singled her out, but the few times he'd attempted an embrace or to take her hand, other than to help her in or out of his car, she had shrunk from him.

Oh, bother, she thought. *Why can't young men be content with just being friends? Why must they get all sentimental and spoil everything?*

A tiny voice inside spoke up. *If you really loved John—or anyone—you wouldn't feel that way.* Trinity had to admit it was true. What she saw in Letty's quickly hidden gaze contrasted sharply with her own confusion. Shy as she was, if Blakely Butterfield crooked his finger, Letty would follow.

I don't want to think about love until this horrible war is over, Trinity decided. *I only have a few short months to get the Epworth League growing so it can carry on when I go to Cedar Ridge.* A pang went through her but she firmly refused to let it stay.

As soon as church ended, Trinity saw Blakely and John both start her way. She met them in the center aisle, turned, and drew Mollie and Letty into the little circle. "What a fine sermon! Pastor Sullivan certainly has a shepherd's heart, doesn't he?" She managed to chatter until they got into their wraps and stepped outside. "We're all going the same way, aren't we? It's such a nice night. Suppose that we walk."

"I have my car here," John said eagerly. "We can walk another time."

"Oh, all right." Trinity stepped in after Mollie, Letty, and Blakely climbed in the back, glad for Blakely's presence after they delivered the Perkins sisters home. As Blakely held the door open for her, John announced, "I will pick you up after school tomorrow, Miss Mason. I have something especially important to tell you." A few moments later his car purred away into the night.

Trinity and Blakely sauntered up the walk. "I am so glad your parents told the young couple who rented this summer they could only have the rooms until September," Trinity said. She tilted back her head and affectionately looked at the old house that had been home for so long.

"*I'm* just sorry I went off to school before you came," Blakely said. He winced and rubbed his leg.

"Is your wound bothering you again?" she anxiously asked.

"Yes, a bit. If it doesn't heal properly, I can't go back to finish my job." He wasn't to be sidetracked. "Trinity, I know it's brash for me to ask, but do you care for me—even a little?"

"I care for you a great deal, Blakely," she told him quietly, determined to forestall him before he grew serious. "But I don't care for you in the way God wants people to care when they join their lives."

"Could you—sometime?"

"No, Blakely. Although you're older, I sometimes feel you are more my brother Ed's age."

"That's shooting straight!"

To her relief he looked more rueful than heartbroken. On impulse she said, "I know someone very special who isn't that far away but who admires you with her whole heart." She mischievously smiled up at him in the dim streetlight.

"*Really*?" Blakely looked flattered. The next instant he laughed. "Guess I just wanted to be sure you couldn't be interested. Say, who is this girl with such exquisite taste?"

"I'll leave you to find that out for yourself." Trinity's saucy reply made him chuckle again.

"Won't you even give me a hint? After all, it's hard to believe any girl would admire a guy with a bad leg." He glanced down and frowned.

Trinity thought fast. She didn't dare give Letty away, yet would it hurt to plant a clue? "Blakely, look for the sweetest, most sincere Christian girl at church and you'll have no trouble figuring it out." Her eyes glowed. "She wouldn't care if you had no legs. She's that good."

Blakely's shoulders squared. "Then I have to discover who this paragon is. Uh, Trinity, you're not angry about what I said, are you?"

"Of course not, dear boy." She patted his hand the way she used to pat little Albert's.

He burst out laughing. "You're right, you know. In some ways you're a hundred years older than I am. I can hardly wait to see what kind of man it takes to capture you!"

"*I* can wait." She pretended haughtiness.

"Now it's my turn to talk to you like a Dutch uncle," he told her, his eyes gleaming with devilment. "If you don't watch out, you're going to be Trinity Standish before you know it." He ducked her outraged blow and limped up the steps. " 'Nighty-night, poor old lady."

Better for him to laugh than be hurt, Trinity told herself after prayers. "Dear God, he and Letty would be so happy. She would curb his high spirits and he'd add color to her rather drab life in Mollie's shadow. But they're in Your hands." She turned and slept, but not until she muttered, "One down, one to go," thinking of tomorrow's interview with John.

True to his word, John's car panted at the schoolhouse door when Trinity finished her work the next afternoon. Without asking her preference as usual, he swung into a road that led out above Chuckanut Bay. Trinity's heart prayed for help. John Standish was no boyish Blakely Butterfield to be nipped in the bud. Used to having what he wanted when he wanted it, even though she had no reason to doubt his Christian commitment, she could easily lose a good friend unless God sent wisdom in dealing with John.

When he had stopped the car above the shining bay framed in soft hills and blue sky he said, "I'm leaving for Canada tomorrow."

"*So soon*?" Surprise gripped Trinity and her heart pounded. Perhaps she cared more than she realized.

"Father and the ranch need me. Now that I've finished my special studies here in the States, I must go back. Miss Mason—Trinity—if you loved a fellow would you give up your American citizenship and follow him to his country as Ruth followed Naomi?"

Trinity didn't answer for a long time. Suddenly she felt as old as Blakely had called her teasingly the night before. She liked him tremendously. If she consented to be his wife she knew he'd generously allow her to make things easier for those at home. She'd never have to teach again. Her eyes widened at the thought. *Never teach*? Never again know the joy of sticky fingers on her arm, or the earnestness of trusting faces? Why, it would be like dousing the torch Grandma Clarissa once handed her into icy water!

John suddenly said, "I can answer my own question. If you really loved someone you would be a Ruth, wouldn't you?" His wheatened hair glistened in the late afternoon sunlight and he took her hand. "Can I ever be that man, Trinity?"

Compelled to painful honesty, she looked straight into his hopeful eyes. "I don't know."

Something leaped into life, a triumphant but hesitant look. "Haven't you had enough time? You asked for time when you went back to Cedar Ridge for the summer." Anger flushed his fair skin. "You aren't just keeping me dangling, are you?"

"Certainly not!" She tugged her hand free, furious at the absurd idea.

"I'm sorry. It's just that I care so much for you."

"John," Trinity said as she straightened her shoulders and took a deep breath, "until this war ends I can't even consider falling in love or becoming betrothed. I've told you I like being with you and see wonderful qualities in you. But that's all. If I have to give an answer, it's no."

The color left his face. "I don't want that kind of answer and I regret my impatience. I know that even if you cared the way I hope you will one day you're committed to teach the rest of the year in Cedar Ridge." A tiny smile lightened his features.

Did he think she was bound to contrast the unlearned and rugged men in her hometown with his polish? She glanced down to hide her annoyance at such an idea. Rugged they might be, but no men or boys on earth were finer than those who tilled the land and took their living from the forests. She hadn't known until that moment how strongly she believed it.

"Can't we just be good friends, John?" she asked.

"Not forever." He started the engine but managed a smile. "You'll write, won't you?"

Reprieved, she quickly answered, "Of course," and led the conversation back to lighter topics for the ride home.

To Trinity's amusement, Blakely began a serious search for his secret admirer immediately. At Thursday night prayer meeting he scanned every face until everyone knelt for prayer. Afterward he continued his spy activities and chortled when he and Trinity arrived home. "I don't know who it is but I know some girls it isn't."

"Really?" Trinity's brows raised at his assurance. "Who and how?"

"Well, it isn't Mollie—she's too busy thinking about how she looks and if her frills are straight. It isn't Fan or Beth; they whispered all through the prayers and you said my girl is sincere and Christian all the way through. I overheard Sally making a cutting remark about the way Tim prayed so it can't be her."

"Excellent, dear sleuth." But Trinity gave no more hints.

She didn't have to. When Letty recited her Scripture verse by heart on Sunday night, her brown eyes glowing with excitement, Blakely cocked his head to one side, searched out Trinity's laughing gaze, and slowly nodded. He crossed his arms and a satisfied smile—not unlike that of the infamous Cheshire Cat—spread from ear to ear.

"Am I right?" he demanded in an undertone between Epworth League and the Sunday night service.

"I can't say." Trinity pressed her lips together to keep from laughing.

"You don't have to." He turned. "Miss Perkins, may I see you home tonight?"

To both his and Trinity's dismay, Mollie eagerly cried, "Why, of course, Mr. Butterfield."

"Get me out of this," Blakely pleaded the moment church ended and he could sidle next to Trinity. "I want *my* girl, not Mollie."

"And since when has Letty been *your* girl?" Trinity teased.

Color rose from the sailor collar to Blakely's hairline. "I—I think she has for a long time but I just didn't know it."

With her usual tact, Trinity gathered a group who all lived close and saw to it that she took Mollie aside for a private word on the way home. "Isn't it splendid that Blakely has finally discovered Letty?" She slipped her arm through her friend's and kept her voice low. "Thank goodness you spoke right up for her tonight! She's so modest I don't know if Letty could bring herself to accept even though it's obvious how much Blakely admires her." She felt Mollie's involuntary jerk then Mollie's quick wits took over.

"You are *so* right. That sister of mine is sweet but she's never had what you call a special beau." Mollie gained assurance as she spoke. "You really think Blakely's serious?"

"Just between us, I don't see how he could be more serious," Trinity said honestly. "By the way, when Tad Thorson asked tonight for us to write him—you know, he leaves soon—did you notice how he looked right at you?"

Mollie's face shone in the moonlight. "Why, no, I didn't." She laughed a little self-consciously and played with a blond curl that had escaped her close-fitting hat. "He's new and I don't know him very well yet."

Trinity turned her head to keep from laughing at the word *yet*. Trust the lovable but featherheaded Mollie to add that.

Two hours later she lay in bed, well pleased at the results of her Machiavellian schemes. Great happiness lay ahead for Blakely and Letty in spite of the war, and Mollie had been successfully sidetracked from possible interference by a pursuit of her own. Now she could concentrate on her own problems! She had missed John greatly even in the few days he'd been gone. Did missing him signal a deeper affection than she'd suspected?

Trinity tossed and turned, reducing her pillow to a

lumpy mass before deliberately shutting her mind to wheat ranches, social position, Canadian citizenship, and John Standish. Only God knew her heart and, at least for now, He wasn't telling what might be buried there.

five

Now that John had gone back to Canada—and Trinity wore no ring on her engagement finger—other young men hastened to fill the spot by her side. She treated them all alike, to Blakely Butterfield's enjoyment. Secure in his growing courtship of Letty, he became a self-styled expert in matters of the heart and never missed a chance to give Trinity the benefit of his newfound wisdom.

"I always say," he began ponderously one evening when they arrived home from church, "girls should keep men guessing." He dropped to a chair and grinned up at Trinity who stood by the door.

"Letty will be eager to hear that, I'm sure," she retorted.

"Hey, wait a minute! Not Letty." He scrambled up and had the grace to laugh. "She doesn't need to keep me guessing and she won't after Thursday's prayer meeting."

Trinity abandoned her teasing. "Why not?"

"This is why." Blakely slowly took a tiny box from his pocket. "I wanted to give it to her tonight but I couldn't get her away from the others." He pressed a spring. "Think she'll like it?"

How boyish he continued to be, in spite of the horrors of fighting that sometimes lurked in his eyes. How eager he seemed that the sweet girl he'd overlooked and now worshiped only next to his Lord would like his gift.

"She said once she didn't like diamonds so I thought

she'd like my great-grandma's ring. It's a forget-me-not, see?"

Trinity's throat felt tight when she held the simple worn golden band with an enamel forget-me-not surrounding a small but perfect sapphire on top. "It's beautiful."

"I haven't forgotten who helped open my eyes to what was there all the time." He squeezed Trinity's hand in a comradely fashion. "Someday I hope you'll find someone as special as Letty." As he released her hand he managed a little laugh. "No doubt of that. I'll bet somewhere right now a certain someone is wondering who God has in mind for him, never knowing or even suspecting it will be Trinity Mason."

Tears blurred the girl's eyes. "Thank you, Blakely." She turned and fled. Why should a hazy image form in her mind, not of John Standish, but a stranger whose face she could not see? Yet, how could such a person find her once she moved back to Cedar Ridge? All things were possible with God, but no one in the little mountain hamlet fit her ideas of a lifetime mate!

Under Trinity's leadership, the Epworth League thrived. Within weeks, eager members had brought in friends by ones, two, and half-dozens, determined to be on the winning team and be honored at the monthly socials. The newcomers came, returned, learned Bible verses, and brought others. When time came to tally the scores, to everyone's amazement the winning team had only one point more than their good-natured competitors!

Trinity's eyes sparkled when she made her announcement. "If the weather holds, next Saturday will be an all-day outing. Our host team has arranged for launches to take us across Lummi Bay to Lummi Island. This may well be our last outdoor picnic for a while so make sure everyone's invited."

Saturday came cool and overcast but warm enough for the eager group. Laughing and joking— "If we stayed home every time it clouded up in Washington we'd become housebound!"— but above all, eating, the day sped by. Trinity observed the results of her faithful friends' efforts with a bittersweet ache in her heart. Although so many new faces surrounded her, the empty spaces that should have been filled with men now overseas were obvious. She thought of Ed, still at Camp Lewis baking hundreds of loaves of bread in the monstrous ovens. Thankfulness went through her but shame quickly replaced it. How could she rejoice that her brother remained safe when many here had brothers and sisters even now in grave danger?

By midafternoon the leaden sky began to leak. Big, single drops were followed by an absolute deluge.

"Into the launches," Pastor Sullivan ordered with an anxious look at the scowling skies. Trinity and the others quickly gathered blankets, picnic baskets, and sweaters. Long before the last nose count to make sure everyone was present, the launches tossed wildly at their moorings.

"I—I'm afraid," Letty whispered to Mollie and Trinity.

"So am I!" Mollie clung to her sister.

"It's all right," Trinity forced out between clenched teeth. The friendly waters that had offered salty coolness just hours before when the girls trailed their fingers over the side of the boat had changed to an angry enemy.

Greedy, sucking waves made hard going and even the best prepared were soaked.

Miserable, frightened, and thoroughly upset, the band of pleasure seekers crouched low in the launches until Blakely took things in his own hands and yelled above the storm's roar. "Well, if you losers are such poor sports you didn't want to give us a party, why didn't you just say so?" He waved at their grim surroundings. "I mean, this is really going to pretty drastic lengths, isn't it?"

A moment of startled silence then laughter followed.

"Come on, friends, let's sing," Trinity called.

"What?" shouted those in the other boats.

Undaunted by a wave that dumped icy water over them, Blakely cupped his hands around his mouth and bellowed, "What else? 'Jesus, Savior, Pilot Me!' "

Trinity clung to Letty and laughed until she cried but Mollie's clear voice rang out, soon followed by others. Amid the cresting waves and beating rain, their singing rose.

In the semidarkness of the storm, the launches at last reached the mainland. Pastor Sullivan hurried the drenched but happy crew into waiting cars and raised his hand in blessing. "Thank God for His goodness and care."

A chorus of "amens" echoed in the lowering fog but Blakely had the last word. "See you all in church," he cried, and slid in beside Letty, who now proudly wore his forget-me-not ring.

"I n–never saw anything that looked so g–good as the l–lights on the shore," Mollie chattered and scooted a little closer to Tad, their driver.

"You never appreciate light until you are in darkness,"

Tad told her. "We just take it for granted until it's gone. Or maybe we don't think about it at all."

Trinity caught something in his voice that made her heart quicken. She quietly said, "That's why it's so important to let Jesus be our light." Before Tad might feel uncomfortable she added, "Speaking of lights, what I want right now is my own well-lighted room and a hot bath, if I can beat Blakely to the bathroom!"

"Don't I always let ladies go first, even when it means bathing in a flower-scented room?" he demanded.

"Usually, except when it's time to pick up Letty," she retorted, but their arrival at the Perkins home ended the argument.

Later, ensconced in her bed, Trinity reflected on the day. What had been said about light and darkness fit in so well with Grandma Clarissa's little sermon all those years before. Mingled with her reluctance to leave Bellingham, she found a tiny spark glowing, a curious, eager wondering at what life in Cedar Ridge would bring. All eight grades in a one-room school? How many classes was that in all? She drowsily ran over them: reading, writing, arithmetic, history, geography, spelling, and science and nature. Seven subjects times eight grades . . . .

She sat bolt upright in bed. "*Fifty-six classes*? *Impossible*!" Trinity fell back against her pillows and pulled warm blankets high under her chin. "Dear God, if You want me to hold a torch for You in that one-room school . . . ." She drifted off to sleep before finishing.

One Thursday morning in late October Trinity came home from school rejoicing. She had the next day off due to a fault in the heating system that must be fixed. "I'm going home for the weekend," she told a surprised Mrs. Butterfield, and quickly sorted out what few clothes she'd need. No use bothering with house dresses; she still had old dresses in her closet at home. The suit she traveled in and a middy outfit would do. By the time Blakely brought the family car around to take her to the train station, she was ready.

Although the Butterfields had invited her to spend Thanksgiving with them, Trinity's farewell to Blakely seemed somehow final.

Blakely covered her hand with one of his. "You know we don't want to lose you but just think of the opportunity you have in Cedar Ridge. I remember you saying the church there doesn't have much for the young people yet. Maybe God knows they need you even more than we do."

Trinity gathered her skirts and stepped from the car. But on the long journey she considered his words as she gazed out the window. How many of the glorious colored leaves held on to their secure position on branches, she thought. Only when a strong breeze came along did the leaves swirl and float down. *They're a lot like me*, she mused, *they cling to the familiar*.

All day Friday and Saturday Trinity helped at home. Mama had grown rounder and rounder; the new baby would probably come before Christmas. Late Saturday afternoon Faith burst into Trinity's room. "Come on, it's a long walk to the party."

Trinity smoothed her navy skirt and middy blouse and adjusted a white tie she'd added. "I don't know why I'm going. I don't even know the Thatchers. They moved in after I went away to school."

"I know you'll love them." Faith's bright face encouraged her sister. "I'm so glad I get to board with them during the week now and come home weekends. I adore my school— but it's a real challenge."

"That's what I'm afraid of," Trinity sighed, but obediently got into a warm coat for the long walk. Unwilling to dwell on the future she asked, "What's the party for?"

"It's a surprise going-away party for the oldest son Will. His draft papers are due any minute. The old ranchhouse will ring tonight." Joy left her face. "I wish this war would end. Every time mail comes I dread hearing for fear some of our boys will be listed killed or missing."

A tiny bell rang in Trinity's mind. "Faith, is there someone special—for you, I mean?"

Faith turned toward her sister and beamed shyly. "A good friend of the Thatchers, Donald McKenna." She laughed shakily. "Oh, I'm a couple of years older than he and I don't know if he would ever look at me but I can't bear to think he may be called." Desolation filled her voice and she wiped her eyes with the back of her hand.

"It's selfish to think of my feelings when others have so much more to face. Just a few weeks ago the Thatchers' second son Daniel was killed in a logging accident." She quickly sketched in the details for Trinity. "He died in Will's arms."

"Oh, no!" Compassion flooded Trinity's soft heart. "How could he stand it?"

"Through the faith in God and His Son that has been the foundation of generations of Thatchers." Respect shone in Faith's eyes. "I've never seen such a family outside of ours that relied on the Lord for absolutely everything. Why, even if the hay isn't all in on Saturday night and a heavy rainstorm is predicted, no Thatcher works in the fields on Sunday."

Trinity's eyes opened wide. "Really? What do they do about wet hay? It molds, doesn't it?"

"Believe it or not, the Thatcher hay never gets wet on Sundays." Faith's eyes twinkled at the look in Trinity's face. "It rains all around their place but not on their hay."

"I've never heard such a thing," Trinity gasped and almost stumbled over a rock in the road.

"It's true." A worried frown marred Faith's pretty face. "I am concerned over Will, though. He wanted to go to college and become an engineer but because he's the oldest son, he could only finish tenth grade."

"Sounds like quite the paragon." Trinity wondered at her flip reply. *Didn't she know how it felt to be bound one place and long to be another?*

"He's a fine young man. Sensitive, handsome, a real gentleman."

Trinity's lip curled. "A gentleman logger? My college professors would have trouble believing that."

"Not if they met Will Thatcher," Faith sturdily insisted.

"How can you be interested in this Donald McKenna with your Will Thatcher around?"

Faith threw back her head and laughed. "Not *my* Will Thatcher, worse luck. Even if I hadn't picked Donald I wouldn't get any ideas about Will. Practically every girl up and down the Skagit Valley and around Cedar Ridge has set her cap for him. He is absolutely *the* catch in these parts."

"How does he feel about the girls, the ones who chase him?"

Faith shrugged. "According to Ellen and Rachel, his sisters, he likes them all. Takes one to one party, a different one to the next. He's a real loner, though. Never lets anyone get too close. After Daniel died, he had it really rough. It took time for even Donald with all his charm to get through and become Will's close friend." Faith paused a minute. "Any time a girl tries to drop a halter on Will, he gracefully slides away."

"So what is it that intrigues all the girls? His remoteness? Or is he some kind of modern Pied Piper, conceited and unbearable?" Trinity's curiosity was piqued.

Faith's eyes flashed fire. "Absolutely not! I've never known a more unspoiled young man."

She sounded hypnotized by Will Thatcher! It wasn't like Faith to rave about young men. Well, bring on Mr. Ideal. Trinity tossed her proud head. At least one girl wouldn't follow after him like a pathetic lamb. Yet she couldn't help feeling a little pain at the thought of the young man who held his dying brother, powerless to do anything.

In an effort to overcome her mixed feelings, Trinity begged, "Tell me more about your school. How *do* you handle all those classes?"

"It isn't as hard as you'd expect. The older ones hear the little ones reading lessons while I work with another group." Faith's whole face came alive. "I have twenty pupils this year so I have just a few in each grade. These children really learn. When the older ones hear the younger pupils' lessons, they benefit; likewise the young ones benefit from the discussions among the older pupils." All the rest of the way to the Thatcher farm Trinity questioned and Faith answered.

When they reached the well-lighted ranchhouse, people of all ages spilled from the doorways. The light from freshly polished kerosene lamps and the roaring fire in the fireplace was complemented by the good smells of country cooking.

The Thatchers themselves were warm and welcoming. Trinity would never forget her first encounters with them: Mr. Thatcher and his drooping mustache and bright blue eyes; busy Mrs. Thatcher among her pots and pans; Curtis and young Andrew, Ellen, and Rachel all mingled into a happy, laughing crowd.

"Where's Will?" Faith asked and craned her neck to scan the group.

"Out riding, as usual," Rachel piped up. "Ma says he'll be back soon."

With the arrival of more guests by horse-drawn wagons, on foot, and in a few well-loaded cars, came a few uniformed men. To Trinity's surprise, a sailor and a soldier she had briefly met the summer before soon sought her out.

"Why, Miss Mason!" Delight showed on their well-scrubbed faces. "What a nice surprise." The soldier sat down on her right and beamed. "May I show you the family album?" He reached for the inevitable pictured record on the small table next to the couch.

Not to be outdone, the sailor who had immediately grabbed the vacant spot on her left asked, "May I get you a cup of punch, Miss Mason?"

"Thank you. It's a thirsty walk out from Cedar Ridge,

isn't it?" Trinity smiled, all thought of the missing guest
of honor driven away by the unexpected meeting.

Head bent over the album, Trinity idly flipped pages
wondering who the people in the pictures might be.
Then a little ripple ran through the crowd. She raised her
head and glanced at the staircase off to one side of the
room. A young man appeared at the top and came down
two steps at a time. This was no suit-clad man, but
neither did he wear a uniform. His dark blue flannel
shirt, open at the neck, exposed a tanned throat. Jeans
covered a slim waist and lean legs. Over six feet tall, not
an ounce of fat marred his strong body.

Trinity looked into his face. Golden brown hair lay in
ripples and his wide mouth stretched in a laugh that sent
sparkles into eyes as blue as her own.

Something happened inside Trinity. A strange sense
of familiarity for the stranger left her unable to look
away from the penetrating blue eyes that held surprise
and something else she couldn't define. A swarm of
friends surged between them and she tore free her gaze.

"Who is *that*?" she demanded of her self-appointed
escorts, knowing the answer before it came yet unwilling to admit it. "I must be the only person here who
doesn't know him."

"Oh, haven't you met Will Thatcher?" The soldier
flipped album pages. "I thought everyone knew Will.
Nice chap."

Trinity recalled Faith's earlier words of praise for the
young man who had looked at her so intently yet with
respect and almost reverence.

Don't be a fool, she ordered herself. *What are you to
him or he to you? You are a grown woman who will soon*

be responsible for an entire school, not a schoolgirl meeting the new boy in class!

Yet when someone slid into the empty place at her left and she observed through downcast lashes dark blue jeans instead of sailor trousers, Trinity experienced a moment of total panic unlike any emotion she'd ever known.

six

Her mind gone blank, Trinity stubbornly stared at the floor until the tips of two highly polished shoes stepped into her line of vision. A voice barely suppressing outrage said, "Here's your punch, Miss Mason."

She forced a smile and looked up. "Why, thank you," she said, when she wanted to laugh out loud. Never had she seen such a frustrated young man as the sailor whose place by her side had been claimed in the few minutes he'd been gone. This was a trick worthy of John Standish!

Trinity sipped the ice-cold punch, glad for its coolness in the suddenly too-warm room. The soldier on her right made a noble effort to regain her attention by turning more album pages when an amused voice cut in.

"It would be easier for me to explain the photographs to Miss Mason since it's our family album." Will Thatcher's smile took any possible sting from the words and he held out his hand for the album. The soldier's glare matched the sailor's but he had no choice but to hand over the heavy album.

Trinity's heart beat faster. So this was Will Thatcher, and he was everything Faith described—and more. Faith hadn't told of the innocent mischief that sent twinkles in the blue eyes and made Trinity part of his little ploy. Neither had she predicted how his smile took away a girl's breath and made her stomach turn upside down. Trinity had never believed in love at first sight and yet . . .

"Will, Will!" A nightgowned urchin dashed into the room and hurled himself into open, welcoming arms.

"What are you doing out of bed, Bruce?" Will held the small boy up in both strong hands.

Trinity noticed how much little Bruce resembled Will from the lake-blue eyes and soft golden ringlets to the totally enchanting smile. "He's adorable! Who is he?"

"Miss Mason, may I present Bruce Thatcher, my cousin Jamie's boy? Here comes his mother now." He nodded to a charming brown-haired, brown-eyed young woman who had stopped to chat with Ellen and Rachel. "Bruce, this is Miss Mason. She's Miss Faith's sister."

"Ooh, you're pretty!" He stuck one finger in his mouth and beamed up at her.

"And you're handsome," Trinity told him gravely. Bruce giggled and showed small, pearly teeth.

"You're a scamp," Sarah Thatcher announced, and reached for her son. Her merry eyes denied annoyance at Bruce's antics.

Trinity shared a look with Sarah that won her over completely. Of all the girls and women she'd met, only Letty and Mollie had earned her deepest friendship. Yet she knew a bond existed between Sarah and her from their first exchange of glances.

"May I go up with you to put him down?" she impulsively asked. "It's been a long time since we had one that age at home—although we will again soon."

"Please do." Sarah smiled at Will. "I'll bring her back."

Will just grinned but Trinity turned as pink as a peony and held her head high when she followed Sarah.

"He's a perfect cherub," she whispered, after Bruce lay tucked in blankets up to his chin, desperately trying to keep his eyes open. "How old is he?"

"Me's fwee," came a high-pitched voice as absurdly long lashes drooped against tender flushed cheeks and sleep came.

"I should have known he'd never go to sleep until he saw Will," Sarah confessed. They tiptoed out into the hall. "He's crazy about Will, has been ever since he could recognize people. It's not surprising, though. Everyone loves Will." Her smile was gentle and quick. "I'm so glad you came. Will needs someone—"

Before she could finish her sentence that had already sent warm blood pumping through Trinity's veins, someone called, "Come on, you two! We need you," and the evening's simple games and fun claimed them.

Was it coincidence that in every game Will just happened to be her partner? Trinity wondered. Near the end of the evening the Thatchers brought out musical instruments and the party ending with singing. Faith at the piano, Will strumming his guitar, and Thatcher cousins with fiddles and a mandolin made the rafters ring. Trinity closed her eyes. She was almost back with the Bellingham group! They closed their parties the same way. Her eyes opened wide. Strange, the permanent ache over having to leave her city friends had disappeared in the gaiety and genuine welcome of these Cedar Ridge folks. With Will on one side and Sarah and her Jamie on the other, nostalgia had no place.

Then a terrible thought intruded. *I've just met him but this is his farewell party. He's going away to fight. I may never see him again.* Trinity felt shaken and confused. Why should the idea upset her so? She wanted to cry out against this war that demanded the sacrifice of America's brightest and best. When the time came to stand and sing the beautiful farewell blessing, "God be with you till we meet again," not one word could get through Trinity's constricted throat. Upstairs little Bruce lay sleeping, secure in his family's love. Downstairs his beloved Will prepared to answer the call of his country. It took every bit of control Trinity had to hold back tears with the last note of the song. Around her she saw tightened lips and misty eyes of the others who shared her feelings.

Will broke the emotion-charged moment. "Thanks, folks. If I'd known you were coming I'd have put on a suit and high collar." He ran tanned fingers around the open neck of his flannel shirt. "Have to admit, this is a lot more comfortable."

"You can say that again," said Donald McKenna, crossing his eyes, his tongue hanging out. "Being polite sure is painful." The burst of laughter eased the tension.

Those with small children left first. Bruce opened one sleepy eye and said, " 'Bye, Will. 'Bye, pretty lady. I like you."

Trinity hugged Bruce as well as she could with him all bundled up in Jamie's arms. "I like you, too, a whole bunch," she whispered into his sleep-creased neck and felt rewarded when he bestowed another smile on her.

A few minutes later the determined soldier who had kept near her all evening said with a glint in his eyes, "I'll see you home, Miss Mason."

At the same moment the equally stubborn sailor appeared in the doorway with her coat. "I have your coat, Miss Mason. Shall we go?"

Now what? Trinity stifled a nervous giggle and didn't dare look at Will who stood just behind her. She needn't have worried.

"Thank you both, men, but that won't be necessary. Miss Mason and her sister are spending the night here." Will's bland smile and courteous air drew glares from the would-be beaux but Trinity's heart leaped. *When had that been decided*? Surely not before they arrived or Faith would have told her.

She couldn't help pitying the servicemen, both fine young men. "Thank you," she told them. "I appreciate your kindness." She gave each a warm smile and some of the frost in their manner melted.

"We'll see you in church tomorrow morning?" one asked.

"Of course." Will again took charge. "An early morning walk is just what we need after tonight's good food." He showed them out but not before Trinity discovered the little look of triumph in his eyes.

"Well, what do you think of him?" Faith demanded when the girls huddled close in her room.

Trinity snuggled deeper into the warm gown Faith had offered. "Who?" She yawned and pretended innocence when inside she burned to learn more of the fascinating Will Thatcher.

"You know who I mean."

"Oh, Donald. I think he's a grand person and very much attracted if not downright in love with you."

Her diversionary tactics worked. Faith sat up in bed and clutched the blankets to her. "Do you really think so?"

Trinity smiled in the darkness and honestly added, "I do. And if it weren't for this awful war I think he'd have told you long ago. His gaze follows you the way a child follows its mother." She reached over and squeezed her sister's hand. "I'm so happy for you, Faith. You deserve the best."

"So do you." But Faith's voice sounded muffled, as if tears of joy flowed into her feather pillow.

It snowed lightly during the night and then cleared. Early Sunday morning well stocked with a breakfast of ham, biscuits, and gravy, far more than Trinity usually ate, Donald and Faith and Will and Trinity set off for Cedar Ridge.

"It's going to be a long, cold walk for you both ways," Trinity told the others doubtfully.

"It's so beautiful, who cares?" Usually quiet Faith had blossomed overnight. A new softness shone in her eyes and Trinity knew it came from knowing she was loved. A burning blush rose from the fur collar of her warm forest green coat. What if someday Will Thatcher learned to care for her the way Donald cared for Faith? Only by reminding herself Will shied away from girls who chased him could she hang onto her rapidly fleeing dignity.

Never had miles passed so quickly. When Donald and Faith gradually lagged behind, a new worry nagged at Trinity. Would Will try and hold her hand? She hated boys who got spoony yet it would show he liked her.

Will took no liberties but kept up the conversation with a dozen funny stories. Often he pointed out special sights and sounds and smells. "Look," he said over and over. Trinity quickly followed his pointing finger and discovered frisking squirrels, bluejays, and snowbirds, and once a red fox bounded into view, surveyed them, then continued on his way.

Trinity threw her head back and gazed into the inverted blue bowl of sky above them. "But how can you see things so quickly, Mr. Thatcher? I didn't know there was a fox within a hundred miles and then here one came."

"I saw the tip of his ear behind the stump before he came out into the open."

Trinity looked at him suspiciously. He must be joking but his matter-of-fact tone supported his statement.

The farther they walked, the more Trinity wondered about her unusual escort. A spirit of perversity seized her. She'd see how far he'd carry his courtesy. "My hands are cold." Now Will would reach for them, she thought.

"Would you like to put them in my pocket?" He held out the wide, deep pocket of his coat.

"Yes, I would." She slid her left hand in and hid her right hand in her own pocket, not nearly so warm, and waited for Will's hand to clasp her own.

It didn't. Her hand lay in his pocket untouched.

It piqued her curiosity more than ever. Any other man she knew would have taken her hand—and she would have drawn it away!

Donald and Faith caught up with them just before they arrived in Cedar Ridge. Will and Donald were invited in for hot chocolate then all four went to church. Trinity couldn't help but see the envious looks they received, especially from Mamie Arman, one of Faith's girlfriends who prided herself on capturing every good-looking man around. Small and charming, she possessed a grasping nature that demanded attention and soft blond curls that peeped from under her hat. The minute church ended, she attached herself to their little party.

"Well, Donald and Will, how nice to see you! How can

that little church out near your place get along without you for a Sunday?"

The boys grinned and Mamie rushed on. "You must come again." Her music-box laugh tinkled. "And Trinity, we simply cannot wait until you get home." She floated away in response to an urgent call with a gorgeous smile. "Remember, we'll be looking for you."

"Pretty little bit of fluff." Donald's eyes danced.

"If you like fluff." Will's drawl indicated he did not—and his one raised eyebrow did something to Trinity's heart.

"Can you stay for dinner?" Faith asked but Will shook his head.

"No, thank you. Ma already has invited some of the family. I have to get back. Donald, why don't you and Miss Faith stay and come back later? There's no need for you to rush." He lifted his hat to Trinity. "You're going back this afternoon?"

"Yes, I have to teach tomorrow. It's been nice meeting you." She held out her hand.

"And you're coming home at Christmas, for good." A poignant light deepened the blue of Will's eyes. "I'll be gone but have a happy Christmas, Miss Mason. Goodbye." He swung away in his ground-covering stride, leaving Trinity staring after him. She knew then she had lost something precious.

"Oh, God," she prayed that night in the privacy of her room, kneeling by her bed. "Keep him safe. Please, don't let anything happen to Will. Or Donald or Ed," she quickly added.

Later that day Donald kept vigil with his friend. Only he knew that tomorrow Will would go into town and take the train for Camp Lewis, leaving him behind to explain to Will's family.

By the dim light of a dying fire they talked. Donald confessed his hope that Faith did care. "If I go and make it back, I'll tell her. It isn't fair to tie her down for who knows how long." His boyish lips set into manhood. "Say, her sister's quite a girl, isn't she?"

"Yes."

Something in the quiet voice compelled Donald to continue. "Don't get any ideas about her. From what I hear she's the belle of wherever she goes. Besides, schoolteachers are usually a little high-toned, too good for the likes of us."

"Oh?"

Donald blundered on, hating what he felt he must say. "Talk has it every man over eighteen wants to marry her. Faith says she knows of two who are on the verge of proposing in spite of the fact her sister doesn't say much."

"It figures." Will stood from his chair, stretched, and walked to the window. A million stars hovered above the earth as the same number of thoughts crossed his mind. *Will they look the same when I'm overseas fighting?*

At least I met her. Trinity—what an unusual name for an unusual person. He yawned again. Pursued, sought after, and loved she might be, but nothing could take from his heart and mind the look of her vivid face. Beside it every other woman paled into insignificance. The pure blue eyes framed by dark, curling lashes, the white skin that flew bright banners of color when she laughed, and the incredible look when she hugged little Bruce all belonged to Will, to warm the long, cold times ahead.

Did he dare write to her? He set his jaw. *Why not*? Even young Ellen and Rachel sent letters overseas to homesick men, notes of cheer and a taste of home. The little flicker his keen eyes caught in her face when he told her goodbye brought a smile to his carved lips. He just bet she'd answer.

"Dear God, I know You're in charge. You know all about me. Now I ask You to walk with me and help me do what I have to, for the sake of those who are depending on us." He wheeled from the window. "Donald, if you don't come over for a while, look after things, will you?"

Donald poked at the last embers until they briefly flared. "I can't take your place but if ever your family or friends—" he paused. "I'll do all I can." The blaze died, leaving ashes gray as the coming dawn.

The next afternoon Will rode back from town into the yard and leaped from the saddle.

"Why, what—?" The family burst from the house.

"Woooooeeeee!" Will threw his hat into the air and jumped to catch it. "Guess you'll have to put up with me for a while longer."

A babble of questions finally stilled. "There's influenza at Camp Lewis and they aren't taking any more men until they can get it under control. But that isn't all. News is that we've got the enemy on the run and by the time this flu's under control, the war may be over."

"*Thank God*!" Lewis Thatcher's face brightened. "Too many of our men have already been lost or crippled or gassed." A shadow crept over his face. "May God comfort all those who have lost loved ones."

For once the rumors proved true. Peace was realized November 11, 1918, with the signing of the Armistice and in towns and hamlets and cities across the nation the celebration was unequivocal. Even in Bellingham a dark-haired schoolteacher dismissed her class and paraded in the streets with her students in tribute to God and country.

seven

From the exact instant Trinity Mason knew Will Thatcher would not be going away to war, her dread of leaving Bellingham faded. Although she knew she would miss the Butterfields, Letty, Mollie, and the others, she made them promise to come visit Cedar Ridge during holidays and in the summer. Now each day came in a splendor of glory that transcended the rainy November weather and brightened Trinity's smile.

Even when one of her third grade pupils tugged at her skirt and anxiously asked, "Miss Mason, will our new teacher be nice as you?" she only felt a twinge at leaving.

"Of course. She's one of my good friends and her name is Miss Perkins." How fortunate that Mollie finished midterm, she thought.

"But will she love us?" the little inquirer continued.

Trinity dropped to her knees, heedless of crushing her skirt. "How can she help it? I know you and the rest of my class will be as good for her as you are for me."

The early December days passed, marred by the growing specter of the influenza epidemic that had ravaged the world. One of Trinity's schoolchildren fell sick and within days news came she had died. Children lost mothers and fathers and even strong men died. No one knew why some made it and others did not. Trinity dreaded going to school for fear another of the children she loved would fall victim.

A week before the holidays the school board closed

the school until January, freeing Trinity earlier than expected. Bidding a quick and tearful farewell to the Butterfields and promising to write, she caught the train home. With Mama due any minute and a houseful of people who might grow ill, her help was needed desperately.

Would she see Will right away? She fumbled in her dress and took out a crumpled single page. Faith's scrawl showed how hurriedly she had written it. So far Mama and all were well. Jamie Thatcher and Sarah had been sick but Will took charge, sent Bruce to his parents, and nursed his cousin and wife back to health. The doctor seemed a bit dubious about Sarah, who was slow to regain her strength.

Faith finished with, "Everyone helps one another. We haven't lost any but Cedar Ridge hasn't been that hard hit yet. Oh, Will and Vi have become good pals. He stops by when he can."

Vi with her sparkling black eyes and curls might be years younger than Trinity but she was still a beautiful girl. Had Will discovered in his fun-loving "pal" the girl he'd like to court?

Trinity's eyes blazed. If so, no one would hear her whimper. Who was Will Thatcher, anyway? Just a logger, a man who caught her fancy for a fleeting time and had no business taking her attention in quiet moments of remembering. If he cared for Vi, so be it.

Every well member of Epworth League, school friends, members of her class, and many others gathered at the train station to send off Trinity to her new life in Cedar Ridge. Boxes of candy, a few flowers from a hothouse, magazines, and tears mingled in a grand rush of goodbyes.

Letty and Blakely and Mollie held back until the others made way for them.

"Don't forget that you're coming to see me," Trinity told them, her eyes shining.

"Don't *you* forget you're going to be Letty's brides-maid in April," Blakely reminded, and smiled at his girl until Letty's blushes rivaled the few red leaves still hanging on a nearby bush.

"I'll take good care of your class," Mollie promised. Trinity's quick eyes saw the sidelong glance she gave Tad, who stood just a step behind her. She wondered just how long Mollie's teaching career would last! The new softness in her face betrayed far more than the desire to beat someone's time with a good-looking man.

Every inch of railroad track widened the gap between the old and the new. Trinity dreamed her way back to Cedar Ridge. All thoughts, not so remarkably, came to dwell on the only young man she knew who had never tried to hold her hand when he walked with her. Had Will really learned to care for Vi in the short time since the farewell party? Yet when she swung down to the little station platform in Cedar Ridge, her gaze eagerly sought for the laughing man who so quickly had found lodging in her heart.

Will wasn't there.

Keen disappointment shot through Trinity but she managed to hide it amid the attention of her family. Faith hugged her and whispered, "Mama says the new baby will be here soon—maybe tonight or tomorrow!"

Forgetting their schoolteacher status the two raced like young girls down the streets toward the Masons' sprawling, white frame home. The light from a dozen lamps spilled out into the darkening day that heralded snow before morning. In a rush of excitement Trinity almost fell into her mother's welcoming arms and then turned to her smiling father.

Faith chattered far more than usual while the girls prepared supper. Never had Trinity seen her sister so pretty. "Has Donald spoken?" she demanded.

Faith's blushes deepened. "Yes, and Dad and Mama approve." Her quaint wording fitted Faith perfectly.

"I couldn't be happier! Donald McKenna's so in love with you." In high spirits Trinity twitched the bow on her sister's enveloping apron. Then she sobered. "Faith, do—how is Will?" *And Vi*, she burned to add.

Some of Faith's happiness fled and she dropped to the rocking chair that had stood in their big kitchen ever since Trinity could remember. "We haven't seen much of him lately. Jamie came through the flu all right but Sarah's heart was weakened." She frowned. "Dr. Ryan told Mama he wished Sarah would see a specialist but she isn't strong enough yet to make the trip to Seattle."

"I hope she will be all right." Trinity's busy hands stilled among the mound of vegetable parings before her. Sarah's warm, laughing face rose and Trinity recalled their immediate kinship. "It would be terrible if anything happened to her. Bruce didn't get sick, did he?"

"No, the Thatchers still have him. It makes a real burden on Mrs. Thatcher, though. She has so much to do with her own family and neighbors call on her for everything!" Pity sparkled in Faith's eyes. "Mercy, there isn't a family with a sick one or trouble who doesn't eventually wind up asking Ruth Thatcher for help, the same way they did with Mama until a few weeks ago when Doc Ryan roared a mighty, 'No more!' He ordered Mama to stay home until after the baby's born."

The arrival of Ed, who had been honorably discharged from the service, sparkling-eyed Vi, and young Albert, who had been out scouting for *the* special tree to cut, postponed the sisters' confidences. The family was still at the table when Mamie Arman rushed in.

"Hey, everyone, Mama says we can have a little party tonight and you're all invited. Just those who haven't shown any sign of getting this awful flu, that is," she hastily added. A sprinkling of snow on her fetching blue hat made her blond curls prettier than ever. No wonder all the boys admired her, Trinity thought, as she noticed Ed's gaze fixed on their visitor.

Mamie hurried on with her news. "I just happened to see Will Thatcher in town and asked him to come and bring Curtis—and Donald." She sent a roguish glance toward Faith then another at Vi and Trinity. "Hmmm, wonder which Mason girl will be escorted tonight?"

Vi bit her lip and Trinity didn't miss her quick look. Recovering, Vi said practically, "If the boys stop by we'll all go together, as usual." But a pretty rose color crept into her face and her black eyes shone.

Trinity's spirits fell. *So Vi did like Will.*

"I'll just stay over here and walk with you," Mamie announced. She made a show of helping with the dishes and kept up a steady stream of gossip. Trinity said little. Should she plead a headache and excuse herself from the party? No, as a child of God, she had no right to lie just to get out of an uncomfortable situation.

Yet when it came time to get ready she loitered on purpose. Truthfully she told the other girls, "I'm not quite through. You go ahead."

A buzz of laughter downstairs made her feel strangely lonely and left out. How could she spend an evening seeing Will and her charming younger sister together? The very idea made her ache inside. She halfheartedly completed her toilette then crept unobserved to the head of the stairs.

"Come on, Donald, Vi, everyone." Mamie's light commanding voice drifted up to Trinity.

"Where's Miss Thatcher, I mean, Trinity?" a deep voice inquired.

Trinity opened her mouth to cry gladly, "Here!" Will hadn't forgotten her after all. Perhaps he and Vi *were* just pals.

The word never came out. Then Mamie drawled, "Oh, she had to go on ahead and help with some arrangements. Come on, or we'll be late."

Why didn't Faith deny it? From her vantage point Trinity suddenly realized Donald and Faith had already stepped outside, out of earshot. So had Curtis and Ed and the others. Even Vi, struggling into a heavy coat, couldn't have overheard. Only Will and Mamie, out of sight but not out of hearing distance, remained in the hall below.

Trinity shrank back for fear she'd be discovered. A door banged and stillness filled the hall. Mamie with her sneaky tricks! Trinity's blue eyes shot angry sparks. Well, she wouldn't give anyone the satisfaction of knowing she cared one little bit. She noiselessly slipped back to her room. Let them go on without her. Who cared? In a minute she'd go downstairs. If anyone asked afterward what happened, she'd say she decided to spend the evening with Dad and Mama and Grandma Clarissa.

Her face aflame but her heart at peace, after a quick prayer, Trinity swept downstairs, her long skirts trailing behind her. At the bottom she hesitated. A slight movement showed the heavy front door had been left ajar.

Curious to see if everyone *had* left her behind, she opened it and peered out. The scrunch of boots on light snow arrested her.

"Will?" Her throat burned. It couldn't be.

"I'm here, Miss Thatcher. If you'll get your coat we can go," said a voice in the darkness.

Ten minutes later a thrilled and ecstatic Trinity proudly walked into Mamie's party on Will's arm. Although Mamie said nothing of her attempt to steal another girl's beau, Trinity only remembered Will's quiet words.

"Mamie said you'd already gone but I knew better."

"How?" Trinity inquired and held her breath in the snowy night air.

"I know Mamie." A hint of laughter quieted Trinity's doubts and she quickly changed the subject to firmer ground. Further reassurance came when Will casually added, "Your sister Vi's a good little pal, isn't she? Just about the same age as Curtis and pretty as a spotted pony. You know about Donald and Faith, of course?"

"Oh, yes, and we're all happy. He seems to be a fine man." Trinity couldn't keep the lilt from her voice.

"We wondered if she'd ever consider him, her being a schoolteacher and all."

Was there a deeper meaning in Will's statement? Trinity immediately said, "What difference does that make? Schoolteachers don't have to be snobs."

Will's heartfelt, "Glad to hear it," sent shivers through her and she actually welcomed the sight of Mamie's well-lighted porch.

Will never left Trinity's side throughout the party. He claimed her for the walk home and the next evening rode his horse into town, along with Donald and Curtis. A few days later after Dr. Ryan delivered a lusty son and Mama named him Robert William, Will paid another visit, bringing a basket of fresh oranges he had sent in on the train.

"Mighty fine name," he told Mama.

Her eyes twinkled back. "Vi got hold of a book of names and we found out Robert meant 'bright fame' and William meant 'determined guardian' so we figured our son couldn't go wrong with those names."

Trinity caught Will's look before he lifted his eyebrows in a droll way. "Determined guardian. A girl might like that, don't you think?"

Mama innocently replied, "A girl might," as Trinity made an excuse to leave the room to hide her burning face. Will found her busy in the kitchen when he had to leave and contented himself with merely saying, "You have a fine new brother." But his eyes held a poignancy that remained in Trinity's heart and mind long after he had gone. She walked around in a glow until the next day when Albert came back from the general store that also served as a post office.

"Letter for you." He danced around his big sister's chair and tantalizingly held it just out of reach.

"Give your sister her letter," Grandma Clarissa quietly said, and Albert tossed it in Trinity's lap.

She picked it up and quickly stood. "I'll read it

upstairs."

"Why?" Albert tormented in typical fashion for his age. "What's Will gonna say when he learns you get letters from *Canada*?"

"I can't see why he should even know unless certain people can't keep still about things that don't concern them."

"Aw, Trinity, I didn't mean to make you mad. You know I don't tattle."

She relented enough to give him a friendly grin then ran upstairs and with trembling fingers opened the letter. She read it and then read it again.

> *Dear Miss Mason or Trinity, as I think of you,*
>
> *It seems years rather than months since we said goodbye and I came back to my wheat ranch. My kingdom seems to stretch as far as I can see in all directions. I have all the money I will need for a lifetime and enough to leave my sons and daughters for their lifetimes.*
>
> *My darling girl, my kingdom lacks only one thing: a queen to rule my heart and reign over it. I plan to come to Cedar Ridge very soon. I am bringing a ring for you and hopefully one day in the near future my empire will be complete.*
>
> > *Devotedly,*
> > *John Standish*

"Oh, no!" Trinity let out a cry of pure horror. Visions of the scorn and fury Will's expressive eyes would surely hold if he knew about this letter rose and accused her. A wave of anger followed. *What right did John have to send such a letter*? She had made no promises to him. She owed him nothing.

Before her fury could recede, she snatched pen and paper to write back in no uncertain terms what she thought of him.

Yet the ink dried on the pen point and the right words eluded her. She had liked John and he couldn't have helped knowing it. Any coy reply or less than direct answer would simply whet his determination to a cutting edge. She must stop him from coming to Cedar Ridge at all costs. The tendrils of friendship and something more had only begun to entwine her and Will. John's arrival could tear down those fragile strands.

At last a mischievous smile crossed her face. She hurriedly began to write:

> *Dear John Standish,*
>
> *While I am flattered by your offer and appreciate the great honor you have paid me, I am afraid that a visit from you would be inappropriate.*
>
> *You see, I am to be married, so your coming here is sure to prove awkward.*
>
> *Again, let me thank you for your respect and affection.*
>
> *Your sincere friend,*
> *Trinity Mason*

She hastily addressed an envelope and stuffed in the letter. Before she could seal it, Faith came in.

"Albert said you got a letter from Canada." The statement sounded more like a question and Faith's raised eyebrows showed her disapproval.

"*Did I*!" Trinity groaned and handed John's letter to her sister.

"My stars," Faith exploded when she finished it, "how could you lead him on?"

"I didn't," Trinity protested. "He escorted me to church activities but I never, ever, let him think I cared for him more than as a friend. Why, when he asked me to think about it months ago and wanted to know if I ever could care, I told him I didn't know."

"And you know now?"

Her intelligent eyes brought color to Trinity's delicate complexion. "I know I–I don't care for John the way you care for Donald."

"Then you did exactly right except how could you tell him such an untruth and say you are to be married?" Disappointment turned the corner of Faith's lips down. "Dad and Mama have always taught us never to tell anything but the truth."

"It is the truth," Trinity mumbled. "I *will* be married, sometime." She ignored the storm clouds in Faith's face and added, "I can't have him coming here, can I?"

"Well, no." Faith shook her head. "If you're going to mail that, you better do it right away. I'm sure Albert will be glad to run back to the store, especially if you let him know we won't be having a visitor. He's crazy about Will." She ducked a pillow Trinity impulsively tossed at her and fled with a parting shot.

"So is someone else around here if I know people— and I do!"

Trinity devoutly hoped her letter would end John's pursuit. But she wasn't prepared for a second letter that accused her of making a fool of him. She wrote a cold note denying any such accusations and received a broken, apologetic letter saying he had cared too much. This time Trinity didn't reply. Further communication could only result in greater hurt.

eight

A few days before Christmas, Will, Donald, and Curtis arrived bearing gifts. The enormous boxes of chocolates, French creams, and bonbons filled Mama's biggest washtub! The generous trio also managed to get fresh flowers sent, but one bouquet nearly ended in disaster.

Now that the young men came so often to the Mason home, Mamie had practically become a permanent guest. She had obviously set her cap for Will after failing to impress Donald. Even young Curtis and lanky Ed came in for their share of smiles from the fickle and flirtatious young woman.

If she could make a girl miserable, she did. The day Donald arrived with a specially ordered nosegay surrounded by a paper frill Mamie met him in the lower hall. Trinity heard everything from her vantage point in the upstairs hall, scrubbing floors.

"Oh, Donald, the flowers are so beautiful!" Mamie's upturned face showed nothing but innocence and delight. "I know they're for Faith, but there are so many. Could I have just one posy? You don't mind, do you?" She didn't wait for an answer but helped herself to a flower, stuck it in her blond curls, and preened before a mirror. "Oh, thank you so much. I'll tell Faith you're here." She rewarded Donald with a dazzling smile and scurried upstairs. Ignoring Trinity, who was silently counting to ten before calling Mamie something un-Christian, the vain girl lightly ran into Faith's room.

"Donald's here, Faith. He brought you a bouquet."

She twirled and pointed to her hair. From the doorway Trinity longed to snatch down those curls and fling the flower into the ashcan. "Of course, he gave me the first pick." Leaving two speechless girls she bounced back out again.

"Of all the—" Trinity flared.

"Don't mind her," said Faith shrugging, yet a little hurt look crept into her eyes that made Trinity want to cry. Faith's shining love for Donald shouldn't have to be marred by a flirt like Mamie.

"He didn't give her first pick or *any* pick," Trinity raged. "I heard the whole thing and she asked in a way no one could refuse even if she'd given him opportunity. She just reached out and took."

"That's Mamie." Relief erased the doubt in Faith's face. "Reach out and take is her motto."

Two evenings later a similar scene transpired. Trinity had eagerly finished dressing and stood unseen on the top step while Mamie practiced her could-I-have-just-one-posy routine on Will. He carried a sheaf of gorgeous hothouse red roses. This time when she confidently reached out to get a flower Mamie more than met her match. Will held the bouquet out of reach over his head and laughed.

"Sorry, Mamie, these flowers are for Trinity." All Mamie's teasing and fluttering proved useless and Trinity's cheeks rivaled the roses when Will met her halfway up the staircase and presented them to her. Her heart swelled at the way he looked when she buried her nose in their fragrant depths and held them close to her simple white gown.

Mamie pouted and turned her back on them, but

Trinity's keen ears heard her fiercely whisper, "Mean old thing, stingy too." The next instant the tiny beribboned girl vanished toward the parlor calling, "Ed? Are you in here? I declare, it's been so long since we've talked."

Yet all through the happiness of Will's courtship ran the darker strain of trouble. Flu that Cedar Ridge hoped would pass it by descended like the inevitable winter snow. Doc Ryan was run off his feet and often found sleep behind the patient horse that pulled his buggy when some kind of road was available to get him where he needed to be. The rest of the time he rode horseback or walked. One night he rode sixteen miles into the forest to attend one of Jimmy Crowfoot's tribe and found many of the Indian people sick. He did what he could and rode back to Cedar Ridge, gulped a few bites of breakfast, and headed out again.

Fresh mounds that indicated newly dug graves increased. With the logging camps shut down for the winter, Will, Donald, Jimmy, and others spent their time helping where they could. Some farms had every member of the family sick. The young men milked and fed stock while the women prepared and delivered broth and took in children when the parents lay too ill to care for them.

After the Christmas holidays Trinity was faced with parting again from the big, happy Mason household. She would still come home weekends but now she faced the task of teaching all eight grades in the new Cedarton one-room school. Joe Baldwin and his family welcomed her openly and she discovered he'd equipped her new school with everything she needed. The only problem was not seeing Will. His home lay five miles out of Cedar Ridge one way; the Cedarton school was an equal distance a different way. Besides, with the mountains of homework she had to tackle every night Trinity had little time to visit.

However her schedule didn't stop the young bucks on *that* side of the river. Night after night one, two, or more wouldbe beaux appeared on the Baldwin doorstep. Trinity had to excuse herself and seek refuge with her homework in her own little room. Her flight didn't stop jealous neighbor girls from spreading how much attention she had and how many men were after her. The tormented girl silently rebelled, but what could she do? She couldn't order the Baldwins' neighbors out. She just hoped the trouble-makers wouldn't run with their gossip to the Thatchers.

To her own amazement, she adored her new job. The hulking eighth graders who had run out former teachers respected her and worked hard to show how well they could learn and behave. There was little chance that any of them would fail the tough eighth grade state exams.

As Faith predicted, the younger pupils and older ones worked and learned and played together. A quiet word from Trinity quelled any rising rebellion before it burst into a problem. When the young teacher went back to Bellingham in April to serve as Letty's bridesmaid, her last doubts fled.

"I really feel the true meaning of what my grand-mother said so long ago. The children look to me not only for what some of them still call 'book-larnin' but for an example too. We read from the Bible every morning and I make sure to choose verses that will teach how Jesus is with us all the time."

"Have you found your Prince Charming?" Mollie asked as she proudly displayed a diamond ring from

Tad. They would be married as soon as her spring school term ended.

"Perhaps." But Trinity would say no more. To admit the growing love in her heart and soul for one who had not yet spoken might bring her pain if it turned out that Will really didn't care.

How much Will cared became evident a week after Trinity came back from Bellingham. Gap-toothed Joey Baldwin set the scene.

"Mith Mathon, Mith Mathon, there'th gonna be a box thothial."

She hid a grin as she translated "box social." She smiled at the excited child and the others who gathered around her. "That will be fun. Who is it for?"

"Everyone." Big Joe stomped in just in time to hear his son's bulletin. "We'd like to get s'more things for our school so we're asking everyone for miles around." He grinned. "I reckon we can get a good price for *your* basket, Miss Trinity."

A few days before the box social Will unexpectedly showed up just after Trinity dismissed her school.

"Why, Will!" She couldn't keep her pleasure from bursting out.

"Thought I'd ride over and get some information," he teased. "I've got fifty dollars saved up and Donald has the same or a little more. We plan to get our girls' baskets at the box social."

Torn between his comment "our girls" and what else he said, Trinity could only stare. "You aren't planning to spend that kind of money just to eat one dinner with us, are you?"

Will looked shocked. "Of course. That's why we have

box socials, so folks can buy the dinners the girls and women put up in fancy trimmings and eat with someone they like."

Trinity shook her head. "I'm sorry, Will. I'd love for you to buy my box but you need that money."

"You mean you won't tell me what your box will be like?"

"I can't." She twisted her handkerchief. "You'll still come, won't you?"

"I don't know." He sounded doubtful. "The way I hear it, a bunch of the men around here are betting on which one will get your basket. It's too bad, too. They'll spend all their money trying to get yours and a few others and then maybe just offer two bits or so for some of the less popular girls."

She sighed. "Maybe I shouldn't go."

A little smile grew on Will's face. "I have a better idea. You come, but don't tell anyone, especially that talky Joe Baldwin or his wife, what your basket is like." Will touched his horse's flanks lightly with his heels. "See you Saturday night!" He lifted his hat and rode off, his back ramrod straight.

Trinity did exactly what Will said. She locked her door on Saturday afternoon and turned a shoebox filled with fried chicken, potato salad, chocolate cake, and other good eats into a replica of the American flag. Then she wrapped it in brown paper, tied it with string, and smuggled it onto the table with the other gaily decorated boxes and baskets.

Some girls had dressed to match their baskets, including Mamie. Her blue and white checked basket with lacy frills was an easy match with her dress. She crowed when her basket brought ten dollars. One by one the baskets were auctioned off. The modest brown-paper one sold for a dollar to one of Trinity's eighth grade boys. A roar of disappointment went up when he took off the disguise, held up the cleverly designed flag box, and yelled, "Miss Trinity Thatcher!"

Will caught her gaze and raised both hands above his head in a prizefighter's winning clasp. Some of the jealous young men offered the buyer a lot more money to sell "teacher's basket" but he just grinned and proudly led Trinity to a nearby table.

Meanwhile, Will and Donald squelched the plans of some to not spend more than fifty cents for a basket. Every time the bidding stayed low one of them ran it up to at least a couple of dollars. When the auction ended, the boys gathered all the girls and women whose baskets they'd bought, plus some of the boys and men who simply didn't have enough money, and formed a noisy potluck-style group.

"Would you like to join them?" Trinity's escort whispered, his gaze on a pretty seventh-grade girl who kept looking their way.

"If you would."

As he escorted her to the larger group, he won Trinity's devotion. "You're the best teacher we ever had. You make things interesting. I never cared about going to high school before but I do now. Pa and Ma say it's fine."

Spring came in green skirts. Winter snow melted overnight and the land lay soft and new. Gradually the influenza passed, yet new lines lay in the faces of those who lost friends and loved ones. Jimmy Crowfoot's tribe had been cut in half while Sarah Thatcher continued to fight desperately.

Trinity had long since recognized Will's place in her life. Not once since she looked into his blue eyes had she been interested in anyone else and she never would. Likewise, Will no longer visited any girl but Trinity. Sometimes she wondered why he didn't confess the feelings she saw mirrored in the depths of his soul. Perhaps he felt it was too soon. He still carried a lot of responsibility toward his family, as did she.

Even if they became engaged, how could they ever marry when both families needed them so much? Faith also hesitated. Did she have a right to seize happiness of her own when her brothers and sisters needed so much?

One tender moonlit night Will rode up and asked Trinity to go for a walk. He led her to a rustic bridge spanning a small stream silvered by the moon and happily bubbling secrets to its banks. He placed both hands on her shoulders. "Trinity, I have to know. Someday, when things change, will you be my wife? I love you more than life itself and I've never felt this way before."

She had always wondered how the moment of proposal would be, the opening of a heart she realized had been hers since the farewell party. "I will be honored. I've never loved any man but you."

His hands tightened. His gentle kiss held respect, love, and appreciation. There in the moonlight he slipped a diamond ring on her left hand and they knelt together and thanked God. "It may be a long time," he warned. "We both have obligations."

"I know." She ached inside. Now that they were

promised she wanted time to fly. Feelings of resentment filled her, not against their families but against the circumstances that kept them apart. Yet they must not spoil this precious moment by thoughts of the future.

Joey Baldwin was the first to spot the ring she wore to breakfast the next day. "Hey, look at that!" He pointed.

Trinity blushed but held her hand out for inspection. The perfect stone that she knew must have cost far more than Will should have paid caught every glint of morning sunlight. All day her pupils exclaimed over the ring. It made it all seem real, not just a wonderful dream to be interrupted by Joe's lusty yell, "Roll out, everyone."

The Masons and Thatchers exchanged satisfied glances that silently shouted they'd suspected all along. Little by little they considered ways so the young couple wouldn't have to put off their wedding. One Saturday Will burst in and carried Trinity off on horseback to his home. He didn't stop at the house, however, but rode about a mile on down the valley between the mountains to a gentle slope. There a picturesque cabin stood facing the white-capped mountains and overlooking the whole Thatcher spread.

"Old Man Thomas says we can have that cabin if we give him half what we raise," he told her. "It isn't much but we can fix it up any way we like. I'm a good house painter."

"And I can make curtains," Trinity eagerly said. They stepped inside. "How cozy!" She eyed the shabby room seeing it with the floorboards scrubbed, table and chairs painted a bright color with curtain tiebacks to match, and flowers in the window. She peered into the second room. "Oh, big enough for a large bed, a bureau, and—"

"Pa will build cupboards for us," Will promised. "Closets, too. Think you can be happy here?"

"Supremely." She whirled and threw her arms around his neck. "When can we move in?" Her arms fell. "Will? What about our folks?"

"Donald and Faith and you and I will still give something to help them. Your dad says you girls have already done too much, and with the good wages from the Cedarton School they think they can get by. If you don't mind teaching for a little longer we'll make it."

"Of course I don't mind, but is there a school nearby that needs a teacher? I know Faith's going back to hers."

"The White Rock School does need a new teacher, come to think of it. Joe Baldwin's a good sport, so when he knows what we have planned he will fret and fume but he'll give us his blessing." He drew her close. "Trinity, can you be ready by August?"

Trinity thought of her hope chest already filled with handmade sheets, towels, dish cloths, pillowcases, and the like. "I don't have many clothes so if you don't mind a beggar maid coming to you—"

"Sweetheart, someday I'll dress you in silks and satins," he promised grandly.

"I'll settle for gingham and muslin and dimity with some warm woolens for winter," she teased then kissed him. "August it is." She sighed. "Now that it's settled it's going to be hard to wait."

Overnight everything changed. The sound of hooves on an early May morning awoke the Mason household. Trinity recognized Will's voice mingled with a pounding on the door. She tossed on a dressing gown and hurried down the stairs as her father opened the door.

"Trinity," Will gasped, his blue eyes nearly black with urgency. "It's Sarah—she's bad and she wants you. Dress and I'll be back as soon as I get Doc Ryan. We need you, too, sir," he told Edmund.

"Sarah?" Trinity's confused thoughts halted. "How—what—?"

Will had already raced away.

"Go upstairs and get ready, child," her father's quiet voice ordered. "And pray. I doubt if Sarah would be asking for me unless she knows . . . ." His voice trailed off and he disappeared toward his room, leaving Trinity to stumble upstairs and into riding clothing while her heart slowly froze.

nine

The long ride with her father, Doc Ryan, and Will from Cedar Ridge to Jamie and Sarah Thatcher's place remained a blur in Trinity's mind. The tall firs and hemlocks at times reached and joined above the hard-packed dirt road until it appeared they rode in a green tunnel. Trinity tried to pray but found it impossible to get words past the lump of fear in her throat. Yet her rapidly beating heart kept cadence with the drumming hooves. *Help her, help her.*

After they arrived and threw off their coats, Trinity's pitying eyes noticed the kitchen and sitting room. Such disorder spoke eloquently of just how sick Sarah was. Never had such untidiness reigned in Sarah Thatcher's home, although Jamie's rude efforts to brush up were evident. Little Bruce lay disconsolately on his mother's bed, his face tear streaked, seeming to sense his mother's weakness and danger. When the little group came in he sat up and crowed, "Will!" then smiled his enchanting smile as his hero raised him to a strong shoulder and held him perched there.

"Now, now, what's this all about?" Doc blustered.

Sarah had gone downhill rapidly in the few weeks since Trinity had seen her. Thin, pale, and wasted, only her big brown eyes looked the same.

"Everyone out while I examine her," Doc ordered.

"Let Trinity stay." Even the whisper cost Sarah and she took in a deep breath and held it before slowly exhaling.

Jamie's red-rimmed eyes bespoke his anguish as he

105

gently held his wife's hand. So would Will look if it were his wife. He turned at the persuasion of Edmund Mason's hand on his shoulder and together they ambled out the door, closing it behind them.

Doc Ryan placed his stethoscope on Sarah's chest, frowned, and attempted to cover his findings by shrugging. "Not too much change." He busied himself with his worn black bag.

"I want the truth, Doctor Ryan. How long?" Sarah whispered.

He wheeled and squared his shoulders. His gnarled hand lay on Sarah's brown hair in a blessing. "Child, only our good Lord knows that, but . . . ." He pulled a large white handkerchief from his pocket and noisily blew his nose.

"Tell Jamie and the others, but send Bruce to me first."

Trinity gasped. Where had Sarah's strength come from? As she struggled to lean up against her pillows in a sitting position, twin spots of color rose in her cheeks.

"You need to rest now." But little remained of Doc's bark.

"I will, later. Give me five minutes with Trinity then send Bruce in." Something regal in her command sent Doc to the door without another word. Before it closed behind him Sarah turned her luminous eyes on Trinity. "Will you take Bruce for me?"

"I will." There was no hesitation, no pondering what her promise would mean or how she could accomplish it. Her heart had reached out to the young woman who had come to mean so much.

"Then it will be all right." Sarah sagged against the pillows but her iron determination to leave the world as right as she could sustained her. "Jamie will want our son with him nights, but I thought if you'd keep him while Jamie works, perhaps you give them both their supper." Her brown eyes frankly pleaded. "Trinity, someday when it's right, I want you to tell Jamie something for me. I tried but he wouldn't listen. The Thatchers are one-woman-for-a-lifetime men but I don't want my Jamie to live alone for forty or fifty years. Tell him to find another woman, one who will love him and Bruce and perhaps give him more children. We'd planned a houseful." Her lips trembled and Trinity wanted to scream.

"I'll tell him. And Will and I will look after them both, as long as they need us."

"I knew you would. From the first night, I knew your friendship and love could surround me and they have, even when we were apart." A radiant smile highlighted the wan face.

The door opened slowly and little Bruce ran to his mother with outstretched arms. Trinity felt speechless but she mouthed, *Shall I go?* Sarah's almost imperceptible shake of her head sent her to a shadowed corner. She could not intrude on a mother's goodbye. Yet as Sarah talked with her little son, some of the resentment and dread left the trembling young woman.

"Bruce, you've always liked my patchwork quilt. Today I want to tell you a story. Life is kind of like our quilt." She took his chubby fingers and ran them over the many bits and pieces hand-stitched together in tiny but firm stitches.

"Here's a piece of your first little shirt and this is a dress I wore when I first met Daddy."

Trinity marveled at Sarah's steady voice, fascinated at

the story.

"Now, son, Mama has to go away. Daddy and Will and Trinity will take good care of you."

Bruce's blue eyes widened and he put one finger in his mouth. "I don't want you to go."

A bright drop fell on a dark patch in the quilt. "I'd like to stay but God wants me to go be with Him and Jesus. Remember your friend Jesus in the picture?" She pointed to an inexpensive but beautiful artistic interpretation of Jesus surrounded by children.

"Always stay close to Jesus and someday you and Daddy and all of us who love Him will be together again." Before Bruce could answer, she rushed on.

"Bruce, look." She crumpled the patchwork quilt and draped it over her head.

"I can't see you, Mama!" Bruce tugged at the quilt. "Are you still there?"

"I'm here, son. My love will always be here. You don't understand everything now but Daddy and Will and Trinity will teach you more as you grow to be a fine boy, then a man like Daddy." She took down the quilt. "When I go away, you won't be able to see me either, but remember this. I will be close to you as long as you live."

Trinity's eyes spilled over but she clenched her hands into fists and regained control. In no way would she spoil these moments for Bruce—or Sarah.

How much did the solemn little boy understand? He looked at the picture of Jesus and said, "Will you have a little boy where you go?"

Thin arms crept around his sturdy body. "I'd like that."

"Will you love him more than me?"

Trinity thought her heart would break with pain at the childish question but her agony turned to triumph when Sarah hugged Bruce.

"I could never love any other little boy, anywhere, even half as much as I love you!"' Her face glowed with unearthly beauty and her far-seeing eyes shone.

"And someday I'll come?" Bruce asked anxiously. "Daddy and Will and Trinity too?"

"Yes, Bruce. And Grandma and Grandpa and all the others." Sarah silently signaled Trinity in a wordless glance then said, "Go with Trinity, now. Do you know she's going to be your Auntie Trinity very soon?" She hugged him again. "Now scoot and tell Daddy to come see me. Goodbye, son."

" 'Bye, Mama." Bruce accepted Trinity's outstretched hand but patted Sarah's with his other. "I love you."

"I love you too," Sarah whispered.

For their sake, Trinity once more fought tears, knowing she wouldn't have traded those last moments for anything. Her own faith felt renewed as she led Bruce into the other room, now filled with anxious family members and Donald and Faith.

"Ho, there, young 'un." Donald reached for Bruce. "How about you and me going for a walk down to the pond? I saw some brand-new baby ducks there yesterday."

With the ability of childhood to leave one situation for another, Bruce contentedly climbed up Donald and his silver laughter echoed in the room when they went out. Jamie vanished into the bedroom. The others simply waited.

Somehow Trinity felt exalted. Years before her grandmother had passed a torch into her keeping. Today, Sarah had passed a new and different torch, her little son. *God, help me to keep my promise,* her soul cried. *Help me to comfort and nurture this beautiful child You have sent to the Thatchers, and now to me.*

A few hours later Jamie returned to them, strangely at peace. Whatever he and Sarah had shared in that time had given him the same radiance that remained in her now-still face when Trinity and the others went back in for a few moments. In death Sarah's lips still curved in a smile and Trinity remembered a conversation they once had.

"Before I got married I heard a woman say that when she lost her husband, she felt sorry that she didn't treat him the way she wished she had. I made up my mind that I would always treat Jamie with all the love in my heart so if I ever lost him, I wouldn't be like that woman." Softness crept into her eyes. "I have too."

"I know," Trinity had replied, little thinking Sarah would be taken first and vowing the same for herself and Will.

Doc and Dad considerately fell back on the ride into Cedar Ridge, giving Trinity and Will time to talk. She shared with him all Sarah said. "Will, let's don't wait and miss out on time together! We're so young, and I promised Sarah. What are we going to do?"

He slowed his horse and hers and guided them to a grassy patch alongside the road. Dismounting, Will helped her from the saddle to a nearby stump. "I've been thinking all day. I suspected what Sarah wanted because she mentioned it to me, but you had to be the one to agree." He dug his boot heel into the soft earth and stroked a fern. "Trinity, Ma can keep Bruce until you finish in a couple of weeks at Cedarton." He breathed deeply and looked into her eyes. "Will you marry me at the end of May? I know everyone will pitch in and help get our house ready." Blue lights danced in his eyes. "Then you'll have all summer with Bruce." He clasped her hand and she curled her fingers into his strong palm, remembering his laughing comment months before when Robert William was born about a girl wanting a determined guardian.

The strength to meet all the uncertain tomorrows flowed between them. God created male and female to be joined in His plan of marriage and to sustain one another.

"Are you really prepared to take on a four year old as well as a husband?" Will asked. "You didn't bargain for this."

Trinity squeezed his hand. "Will Thatcher, I'd take on a whole passel of children if it meant keeping my promise to Sarah. The only thing is, what about when it's time for me to teach at White Rock School next fall?" She frowned and gazed unseeingly at the swaying wildflowers between the tall ferns. "I don't see how we can get by just now if I don't teach." A thought struck her. "Do you suppose that under the unusual circumstances the school board would agree to let me have him with me, at least for part of the day?"

"I don't know, but it would solve the problem." Will considered for a moment while a magnificent eagle swooped past looking for prey from its aerial vantage point.

Trinity explored the idea further. "He's such a darling

and I know he wouldn't disrupt anything. If I could keep him at school mornings then take him to your mother at the dinner break he'd sleep most of the afternoon and I could pick him up on the way home." The more she thought about it, the more logical it sounded. "Jamie will be coming to us for supper, and—"

"He's already said he won't come unless he can pay," Will told her. "He wants you to figure out what it will cost to feed him and Bruce nights and maybe put up a lunch for him when you do mine. He can manage breakfast for himself but it's too early for Bruce to eat." His brows came together in a straight line. "You'll be up anyway with me, and how much breakfast can a little guy like that eat?"

"We'll work it out," she reassured her tall husband-to-be.

"The only thing that worries Jamie is our not having the privacy newlyweds are entitled to." Will released her hand and slipped his arm around her. Pure mischief replaced his grave manner. "I told him not to worry about that—we'll make sure we spend a lot of time alone. And—" He stopped and held his head back so he could look directly into her eyes. "We don't start keeping Bruce until *after* our honeymoon."

Trinity could feel hot blood flow to her cheeks. "I—I hadn't even thought about that."

"Where do you want to go?" Will waved his hand expansively to include the far horizons.

"With you."

Her simple answer brought an unforgettable look into Will's face, but he teased, "What? No hankering for a trip to Europe or at least to Seattle?"

"You know what I'd really like to do?" She grinned.

"What?" He cocked his head and looked a little suspicious.

"Go camping in the mountains. Find mountain meadows and little lakes. Climb and fish and sleep under the stars." The very prospect of such a trip fired Trinity with enthusiasm.

Will leaped to his feet and pulled her up with him. "My dear, that's just what I had in mind, but I didn't dare propose it for fear you'd be disappointed. There's a certain trip I've wanted to make with you ever since we met—but it's only proper for married couples," he added piously.

"Where? Where?" She hugged him then leaned away to look eagerly into his laughing eyes.

"First Pa takes us up past Darrington into the mountains by car. We have Jimmy Crowfoot meet us at the foot of this trail I know with saddles and pack ponies—he will be glad to do it. We ride up and come to what seems like the top of the world but is really Buck Pass. It's as close to heaven as I've been able to get so far." He cleared his throat but his voice stayed husky. "You can see down the east side of the Cascades to Lake Wenatchee." He held her close and kissed her tenderly. "I'm sure glad God sent me a girl who loves what He created the same way I do."

"So am I." She leaned against his strength. "Will, you asked if I minded about Bruce and I really don't. But what about you? I have to know. I'm the one who promised but it means a different start than you expected too."

His encircling arms tightened. "*Mind*? That little

tyke? Never. I couldn't help thinking all day, what if he were ours and you—" He buried his face in her soft dark brown hair. "Trinity, never go away and leave me, will you?"

What a strange thing for him to say! At that moment Trinity knew what a lonely man Will had been since the death of his brother Daniel. "Never," she whispered and stroked his sleeve. "You're all I ever wanted."

A little later she shared the feeling that came when Sarah entrusted her son's care to her friend.

"If teaching children is carrying a lamp in darkness, then training our own, or in this case, Bruce, is that much more important." A rush of tears threatened but she impatiently brushed them aside. "God gives the greatest responsibility of all when a child is born. Jamie and Sarah have done such a good job. I just hope we can continue what they've started." She swallowed hard. "I know I could never have had the strength to talk with my son the way Sarah did with Bruce, but he will have a memory of his mother to build on. Even if he doesn't remember it exactly—"

"—you'll be right here to impress it in his mind," Will added. "I believe that's why Sarah wanted you to stay in the room, don't you?"

"Yes." Trinity closed her eyes, drained from the day's events yet curiously peaceful.

"Much as I'd like to stay here, we have to get into Cedar Ridge so you can go back to the Baldwins," Will reminded. His bright smile widened. "Things will be different on our honeymoon. Think you can be happy seeing no one but me for two whole weeks, Mrs. Thatcher-to-be?"

Trinity's whole heart confirmed her answer, but she said primly, "I can't think of anything else on earth that would make me happier."

He scooped her up with a shout, placed her in the saddle, then leaped onto his own horse. One shout not enough, be let out a yell that brought the lagging Doc Ryan and Edmund Mason hurrying up the road behind them.

ten

Jimmy Crowfoot squinted at the late May morning sky. His dark face and eyes brightened when Will sauntered over to the corral and grinned.

"What do I owe you for the use of your ponies?" Will asked. He slapped the pack pony's rump and sent it dancing across the packed earth. With experienced eyes he noted the pretty little mare's fine points and stroked her silky mane. "Trinity's going to love her. Is she easy on the road?"

"Single-footer." Jimmy's strong hand rested on the top rail of the fence.

"Good. That's like riding a rocking horse."

As if jealous of the attention given the other horses, Will's own bay thundered up and screeched to a halt a few feet away. "It's okay, Bullet, old boy," Will said as he petted his favorite. "How much, Jimmy?"

"No money, please. Ponies gift." A rare smile highlighted Jimmy's high cheekbones and betrayed his love for Will. But the smile faded when Will asked for advice.

"Is it too early for the mountains? I'd thought we'd be married in August, when the snows had gone." He cast an anxious eye at the distant hills.

Jimmy shook his head. "Skookum horses. Skookum man and woman. Early spring make snows melt. It's okay."

Will heaved a sigh of relief. When Jimmy Crowfoot pronounced something *skookum*—strong and good— Will need not worry. Jimmy had an uncanny way of knowing weather and he had never once been proved wrong in all the time the Thatchers knew him.

"When Will come back, Jimmy get wife." Not a muscle moved to show Jimmy had said anything out of the ordinary but Will shouted with glee.

"Really? Who?"

"Minnie Manyponies make good wife."

Will's hand shot out to grip his friend's. "She's a beautiful girl, Jimmy. I'm happy for you."

"Will come to powwow. Dance with friend."

"Of course." Will successfully hid his surprise at the great honor. To his knowledge, no other white man had ever been asked to dance at an Indian powwow. They could attend only if they treated the ceremony for what it was, a religious celebration. Once when some townspeople had gone and poked fun at the rituals, they were summarily ordered out and told never to come back.

Will's eyes danced with mischief. "Minnie is almost as pretty as Trinity Mason," he observed.

Jimmy guffawed and crossed his arms on his massive chest. "Will Thatcher, listen to story. When Great Spirit make man, He put together like dough then bake in hot sun. First time, man too white, paleface. Great Spirit make new man, bake in sun. Too dark, black man."

Jimmy's eyes gleamed. "Great Spirit make man third time, bake in sun. Man be brown, just right. Indian."

"That's a good story," Will told his friend. "But you know Jesus, God's Son, loves everyone, no matter what color they are." If only he could help Jimmy understand God's salvation!

"Someday Jimmy catch Great Spirit's son Jesus, maybe."

"Don't wait," Will urged. "Jesus loves you, Jimmy, the same as He loves me and everybody."

"Will, why Great Spirit let tribe die?"

Sickness filled the pit of Will's stomach. "I don't know, Jimmy, no one completely understands why those we love have to die." He thought of Sarah Thatcher and of Jimmy's people wiped out in the flu epidemic. "We just take comfort in knowing that if we follow Jesus someday we will be with them again, forever."

"There!"

Will's gaze traced Jimmy's outflung hand toward the horizon slowly brightening into a glorious day that promised to hold.

"B-r-e-a-k-f-a-s-t!"

The call from the farmhouse porch cut short their conversation and Will and Jimmy headed up to get washed for the ample breakfast Ma and the girls had steaming on the table.

"For what we are about to receive, we give You thanks. For Jesus' sake, Amen." Lewis finished the blessing and passed serving dishes of thick-sliced home-cured ham, over-easy eggs, biscuits light as a dandelion puff, rich gravy, and a gigantic bowl of fresh applesauce.

As Will loaded his place, his brother Curtis lifted one eyebrow and said, "Getting married sure doesn't change your appetite, does it?"

Even Jimmy laughed but Will didn't care. "For the next two weeks you can sit at home, pardon me, stay at home and do my share of the work—and think about how Trinity and I'll be eating fresh trout and fried potatoes and—"

"I give, I give." Curtis threw up his hands in defeat.

" 'Course one of these days I may be doing the same for you, that is, when you get old enough and smart enough to make some pretty girl like Vi Mason fall for you." Will calmly reached for another biscuit and the others gleefully pointed to the red creeping up in Curtis's tanned skin.

He got even later. Two mornings from then when Will went to get out his wedding suit Curtis followed, his eyes dancing. "I dare you to wear your clown suit."

"Wha–at?" Will whipped around.

"Your clown suit." Curtis held his sides from laughing. "We're bringing your wedding clothes in the car but you're riding in on Grandy, aren't you? You need something to keep the dust off your riding clothes. Wear the clown suit."

Will's lips twitched. "I will."

"You will? Whoopee!" Curtis yelled and rolled on the floor. But when he finally settled down and his brother stood dressed in the wide-ruffled, spotted clown costume someone had worn for a party, he sobered. "Uh, maybe you shouldn't. What if it makes Trinity mad on your wedding day?"

"It won't." Will adjusted the long sleeves.

"You don't have to. I take back the dare." Curtis looked worried now.

"Too late, little brother. If you're a good sport, though, you'll climb into that old buckskin outfit you wear to hunt in and ride with me."

"*Not me!*" Curtis pulled back in alarm. "Last time we got smart and each wore one red sock and one green sock Vi turned up her nose."

Will threw back his head and roared. He pounded Curtis on the back and crowed, "I knew it!" then lightly ran downstairs and out to the corral. He vaulted up on Grandy's saddle, leaving the rest of the family spilling out into the yard and calling, "Mercy, Will, what *are* you doing in that rig?"

"Going to get married," he flung back. "See you later!"

If ever Cedar Ridge had seen a perfect day, today was it. Once his burst of excitement dwindled, Will slowed Grandy into a steady, easy gait. He savored every foot of his ride to town. How could anyone experience such a morning— one that had started with cleansing dew and had melted into a cloudless sky with fresh-washed flowers and trees, set against rolling land that gave way to low foothills then towering mountains—and not believe in God?

His untrained but perfectly pitched tenor voice rose in praise.

> The Lord's my shepherd, I'll not want.
> He makes me down to lie
> In pastures green. He leadeth me
> The quiet waters by.

The wonderful words of the old Scottish Psalter* mingled with birdsong until Will poured out heart and soul to his Heavenly Father in the last stanza.

> Goodness and mercy all my life
> Shall surely follow me;
> And in God's house forever more
> My dwelling place shall be.

> Shall be, echoed back to him.

---

*From Psalm 23, *Scottish Psalter*, 1650.

Will reined in Grandy, slipped from the saddle, and bared his head. Was this how Moses felt when he stood on holy ground? Too filled with the Spirit of God to consider how ridiculous the clown suit was, Will simply stood silent for a long moment. Back in the saddle he then faced forward toward the girl who would be in his keeping from this day on.

Trinity had also awakened early. She had shared a bed last night with Faith due to the influx of visitors, including Blakely and Letty Butterfield, Mollie, Tad, and the elder Butterfields. Slipping from the bed, unwilling to share these moments even with Faith, she saw with relief that her sister lay undisturbed. Suddenly a pang went through her. Faith and Donald's wedding should have come first.

Was anyone on earth so unselfish as Faith? When she heard the change in circumstances due to Sarah's death, she folded her hands and quietly said, "We can wait until you get back from your honeymoon. It's right that we do."

Trinity blinked hard. If only she could be more like her adored older sister! She tossed a light dressing gown over her nightgown and crossed to the chair by the window. What a day! With a prayer of thanksgiving, she slipped a letter from the nearby desk and reread it in the softly curtained light.

> *Dear sister Trinity,*
> *How happy I am that you have found such a man as Will Thatcher. Mama, Faith, and Vi—even Ed— all have written and confirmed what your letters*

*tell me. I only wish I could be there with you in
body as well as spirit to see you join your life with
Will's.*

*I won't give any advice. I know you well enough
to realize you would never consent to marry anyone you didn't love next only to our Lord, as I do
my husband.*

*Be sure to remember every detail so you can
write to me later. I wouldn't trade my life for
anything but sometimes Panama feels a world
away. I do have some exciting news. If all goes
well we may get home for a visit later in the
summer. Don't tell anyone. If we can't come, we
don't want the family disappointed.*

*Trinity, if you ever discover even half the joy
I've found in my marriage, you will be blessed. I
pray for you and love you,*

> *Your sister,*
> *Hope*

Trinity folded the letter in its original creases and hid
it in the folds of her gown. Will's face swam in the still
morning air, sometimes laughing, often poignant, always filled with love. Humility wrapped her like a soft
quilt. What had she ever done to deserve such a lifetime
companion? Caught in her memories, her eyes flashed
when an incident last night came to mind.

Couldn't Mamie ever say anything nice? Trinity un-
willingly remembered the frivolous girl's parting shot
before she took her tiresome self home and stopped
pestering the bride-to-be half to death. "Well, it's nice
you're getting married," Mamie condescended. "Will's

a good catch." She shrugged in the maddening way she had. "Of course everyone knows when you get a husband you lose a sweetheart," she smirked. "Not me." Trinity prepared to do battle, indignant at the idea. Fortunately, Grandma Clarissa, who continued to be as spry as ever and thought Will the best man in Cedar Ridge, called from upstairs and Trinity left Mamie in the hall.

"*I* won't lose a sweetheart," Trinity whispered. "Oh, I know we'll change over the years but I'm sure Will will always be as much in love with me as I am with him." She stirred restlessly in the chair and Faith moved slightly. "Besides," Trinity whispered again. "I know You brought us together, Lord. With You as the head of our home, we can face what the future brings."

She had only a moment longer to cling to the past, blend it into the present, and leave the future in God's hands. When Faith yawned and sat up in a sleepy trance, Trinity's reverie had ended.

"How long have you been awake?" Faith mumbled.

"Not long." Yet Trinity had the sense of having been awake for an eon; she had seen herself grow upward toward the person God longed for her to be.

"Dearly beloved, we are gathered together . . . ."

Clad in a silky white gown, handmade by her mother, Trinity stared through her misty veil.

Bzzzzz. Bzzzzz.

Good heavens! Why had they decided to be married beside an open window with the climbing, blooming roses just outside?

Bzzzzz. Bzzzzz. A bumblebee, drunk with pollen from

the sweet pink blossoms, dizzily lurched around
Reverend Edmund Mason's head. Not by look or word
did he acknowledge its presence.

Trinity glanced down then stole a peek at Will by her
side, so fine in his new dark blue suit. A muscle twitched
in his cheek and she knew he wanted to laugh as hard as
she.

Bzzzzz. Bzzzzz. The bee divebombed once more then
flew its tipsy way back out the window and into the
roses. Family and friends gave an audible sigh of relief
and Trinity could finally concentrate on her wedding
service.

"Do you, William, take this woman . . . ?"

"Do you, Trinity, take this man . . . ?"

A gold ring slid onto her finger. Will's familiar brown
hands rested lightly on her shoulders as he drew her to
him. "Trinity, my wife," he whispered , and then kissed
her.

Unlike most weddings where the bride and groom
stay to open gifts, Will and Trinity discarded their finery
and donned riding clothes less than an hour after the
wedding. Many miles lay between them and the place
Jimmy would meet them with the horses. Curtis would
ride Grandy back to the ranch.

"I wish Jimmy could have been at our wedding," Will
said wistfully when he climbed into Pa's old car after
ushering Trinity into the middle and leaving the passen-
ger side for Pa.

"It would be right hard for Jimmy to be at your
wedding and still have those ponies waiting for you."
Pa's candid blue eyes twinkled. "Unless he could fly.
Besides, I'll be glad for his company on the way back."

He suddenly got down to business. "Exactly when do you want us to come meet you?"

"Two weeks from today." Will's delighted grin showed all the anticipation Trinity felt.

"Two weeks it is." Pa yawned. "Now if you folks don't mind, I'll catch me a quick nap. We're going to be late getting home tonight." He pulled his hat over his face and tactfully left the newlyweds to themselves for most of the long drive to the meeting place.

"What if Jimmy isn't there?" Trinity ventured.

"He will be." Will slid one hand from the wheel and took hers. "I've never known Jimmy Crowfoot to fail anyone once he gave his word. Wish I could say the same for others."

Jimmy, Bullet, Cloud the single-footer mare, and the pack pony waited at the beginning of the trail leading into the mountains. Pa and Jimmy wasted no time on long goodbyes but headed back as soon as they unloaded the gear. "Two weeks," Pa reminded. "God bless." He raised one hand and put the car in gear. Its motor died away in the distance and Will and Trinity stood surrounded by the green of towering pines, salmonberry, elderberry, and thimbleberry bushes, devil's club, and nettles Will warned her not to touch.

"Where do we go from here?" Trinity's heart beat fast. What did one say to a brand-new husband, anyway?

She settled down when he assumed his role as wilderness guide. Matter-of-factly he said, "There's a good spot just a few miles up the trail, right near a rushing, white-water stream and level enough to set up camp." He glanced at the sun. "We've just about enough time to make it."

How could she feel strange when Will was the one with whom she had begun a new part of her life? They rode hand in hand and the spot he'd described more than lived up to her expectations. By the time they'd eaten the good supper Ruth Thatcher had so thoughtfully packed, darkness threatened. Yet close in the circle of Will's arms, Trinity felt she could face any darkness. "Determined guardian," she murmured, content just to watch the fire die and the stars peer down through the treetops.

"Who, me?" he teased. "If wild animals come around in the night, I expect my new wife to protect *me*." His laugh rang out in the magic clearing. "Haven't you ever heard the story of Betty and the Bear?"

Trinity raised one sleepy eyelid. "I don't think so."

"Well, then, I'll have to educate our schoolmarm," he drawled. Releasing her, he sprang to his feet. "Now I want you to know this isn't the most classy in my repertoire but you may enjoy it." Dramatically, using exaggerated gestures, he recited "Betty and the Bear." *

> *In a pioneer's cabin out West, so they say,*
> *A great big black grizzly trotted one day*
> *To lap the contents of a two-gallon pan*
> *Of milk and potatoes—an excellent meal—*
> *And then looked about to see what he could steal.*
> > *The lord of the mansion awoke from his sleep,*
> > *And, hearing a racket, he ventured to peep*
> > *Just out in the kitchen to see what was there.*
> > *And was scared to behold the great grizzly bear.*

---

*Author unknown.

He screamed in alarm to his slumbering frau,
"There's a bar in the kitchen as big as a cow!"
"A what?" "Why, a bar!" "Well, murder him
then."
"Yes, Betty, I will if you'll first venture in."

So Betty leaped up, the poker she seized
While her man shut the door and against it he
squeezed.

As Betty laid on the grizzly her blows—
Now on his forehead and now on his nose—
Her man through the keyhole kept shouting
within,

"Well done, my brave Betty, now hit him
again.

"Poke with the poker, poke his eyes out."
So with rapping and poking poor Betty alone
At last laid Sir Bruin dead as a stone.

Now when the old man saw the bear was no more,
He ventured to poke his nose out of the door.
And there was the grizzly stretched out on the
    floor.

Then off to the neighbors he hastened to tell
All the wonderful things that that morning
befell;

And he published the marvelous story afar
how

"Me and my Betty jist slaughtered a bar.
"Oh yes, come and see, all the neighbors have
seed it,
"Come and see what we did,
    "Me an' Betty, we did it."

With a final, stagey pose, Will stood statuelike. Trinity pleaded between peals of laughter, "Oh, Will, stop! I ache." She held her sides and rocked back and forth. "Has any bride ever been quoted to like this before?"

When their shared joy dwindled to occasional spasms, Will knelt by her side and took both her hands.

"I never dreamed I could love anyone the way I love you, Mrs. Thatcher," he whispered. "Someday I'll quote other poems, ones about love." Even the dying light couldn't hide the blueness of his eyes. "Tonight I'll just say I've never known such a good pal as well as a sweetheart. I'm just sorry we can't live as long as people did in Old Testament days so you would be my wife for centuries and not just years."

Trinity nodded and said brokenly, "I can't even tell you how much I care, Will." She leaned against his shoulder and the round, white moon poured light into the little glade.

eleven

Trinity sniffed then opened her eyes. Where on earth was she? Gradually she came awake enough to identify her forested surroundings. *Fine thing*, she chided herself. *Sleeping late on your honeymoon.* She scrambled into her warm outdoor clothing wondering where Will might be. Signs of his early rising to provide luxury in the wilderness brought a delighted smile.

A heavy Dutch oven on a bed of coals sent forth the smell of baking biscuits. A string of mouth-watering trout delicately browned above more coals. A coffeepot sang and enticed. Two camp plates, crude cutlery, and tin cups waited on a large stump carefully covered with a cloth. Too tempting to miss, a bowl of wild strawberries almost as large as the ones in the garden at home rested nearby.

"Manna in the wilderness," she exclaimed. If all of married life proved so unexpectedly satisfying, Trinity could ask for no more.

"My goodness! Even a boudoir." She giggled at the pan of hot water, wash dish, new soap, and washcloth and towel on another stump. Glowing from a final splash of ice-cold stream water on her face, she braided her hair into one fat plait that would be out of the way. Will had warned of a long ride ahead.

"Morning, Mrs. Thatcher," Will said eyeing her in approval, his cheeks as scarlet as her own.

"I could have made breakfast." She grinned. "Can't say I'd have provided so lavishly, though. Is it ready?"

"All done but our blessing." He took her hand, bowed his head, and repeated the blessing she'd heard his father give. Then Trinity ate until she was ashamed.

"It's the fresh air," Will excused her, but she caught his delighted grin.

"Of course." She sprang up. "I'll do the dishes while you get the horses ready."

The first morning set the pattern. "I like doing camp cooking," Will insisted. "Once we get home, everything in the kitchen's your department—except for the rocking chair like we have at home. For as long as I can remember, Pa's sat there at the end of the day so he could be with his family before bedtime. He says it irons out the day's wrinkles."

"I like that." Trinity looked up from her dishwashing. She could already picture Will in a rocker in their own kitchen while she set bread or oatmeal for the next day.

"Curtis and Andrew nicknamed our new little home the Doll House," Will told her, busy with bit and bridle.

Trinity clapped her hands. "I can hardly wait to get settled. After our honeymoon, of course," she quickly amended.

Day after satisfying day Will and Trinity climbed higher and higher. Early on the morning after they reached the high country near Buck Pass, the delighted bride awakened to the sound of bells. "What on earth—"

"Sheep," Will told her.

She struggled out of the small tent they sometimes used in the cold, high altitude and brushed sleep from her eyes. "My goodness!"

As far as she could see, flocks of sheep browsed and moved. Gentle *baaas* rose above the tinkling bells. A fine sheep dog, untiring, made her rounds, searching out frisky lambs or strays. "Just like the Good Shepherd," Trinity said, entranced at the wise dog's persistence.

"Ho!" A clear call split the frosty air and a wiry, whitehaired shepherd came toward them, smiling and welcoming visitors to his lofty domain. The peace that comes from working with God's creatures filled his blue eyes and tranquil face and the burr of Scotland touched his tongue. "Will ye be havin' the breakfast wi' me?" he eagerly asked.

Will glanced at Trinity and nodded.

What a breakfast it was with crisp bacon, flapjacks, and rich honey. After they bid their unexpected host farewell, the sole keeper except for the dog of over 1500 sheep, Trinity marveled. "He must get lonely."

"I wouldn't, as long as you were here." The special blue light she loved shone in Will's eyes. She blushed and admitted, in those circumstances, neither would she.

"We'll have to write and tell him he gave us a honeymoon breakfast," she observed but Will laughed and busied himself with taking down the tent.

"He's a canny old man. I'll bet he already knows."

Not a slip of foot or drop of rain marred their mountain trip and on the appointed day when they waited for Pa Thatcher and Jimmy to meet them at the foot of the trail, Trinity sighed. "I hate for it to end. Will, let's come back every year."

"I just hope we can." He gazed longingly back up at the winding, forested trail they'd just descended. His sigh matched hers but he quickly brightened. "Remember, we've the Doll House and Bruce."

"I know and I'm just being selfish." She hugged him. "But if other people weren't involved I'd be perfectly happy to have our shepherd friend's job, at least for the summer."

His blinding smile made her heart flutter.

But all too quickly Will and Trinity were jerked back to reality. Two days after they got home they loaded the wedding gifts the Masons had stored for them, the extra linens for the hope chest, and Will's guitar into Pa's side-curtained car and started for the Doll House.

When they arrived at the ferry to cross the river the ferryman told Pa, who was driving, "Go forward a bit."

Trinity nervously noticed the security bar across the front of the ferry was missing. She held her breath in a dreadful premonition.

The old car rolled forward. Pa reached for the brake, missed it, and hit the gas pedal.

A heartbeat later, the car shot off the ferry, into the river, and sank to the bottom.

Almost before Trinity's mind accepted what had happened Pa Thatcher was washed out of the car and swept away. Will lunged through the side curtains, his iron hands grasping Trinity's full skirts. Coughing and sputtering, he yanked her out of the car and onto the top of the now-settled car. He held her tight against the current that should have been swift and dangerous but now slowly eddied around them. "Thank God the early spring already sent the snow water down," Will gasped.

"Will, your father—" Trinity shook as much from fear now the extreme danger had passed as from the icy river water.

"He's an excellent swimmer." Will's far-seeing eyes

scanned the river downstream and his arms tightened around Trinity.

"Here comes help." In a few moments the Indian ferryman lifted Trinity into his canoe, gave Will a hand in, and rapidly paddled back to the shack he used while on ferry duty. Hot coffee and warm blankets plus the warm June day took away much of her chill. The rest dissolved when Pa Thatcher lunged in, bedraggled but safe.

"Got washed down around the bend, about a half-mile, to the sand bar," he explained. "Trinity, Will, I'm so sorry." Unashamed tears sprang to his eyes. "You've lost all your goods."

"We could have lost a whole lot more, Pa." Will's quiet acceptance of things that couldn't be changed comforted Trinity.

So did the response of the Thatchers and their neighbors. That night everyone who lived near gathered at the Doll House for a surprise party, alerted to the young couple's loss by Curtis and Andrew who rode to the different farms. Every family that came brought what they could ill afford to spare. Trinity had to fight inside to protest the generosity she knew would in many cases cause hardship to the givers. She had caught how Will shook his head when she first realized the extent of her new neighbors' caring. All she could do was to spread wide her hands, murmur, "Thank you and God bless you all," then join with the other women in setting out the variety of food they'd brought and adding what she could to it.

Near the end of the evening, little Bruce climbed into Trinity's apron-clad lap. "Now I get to come here, don't I?"

She realized Jamie and the older Thatchers must have prepared him for his new schedule. "Every day until I start teaching in September you'll be here while your daddy works. Then you get to go to school with me." A fleeting gratitude to the school board who had agreed to the plan touched her.

"I'll still take naps at Grandma and Grandpa's." Bruce's eyes closed then opened then closed again as he drifted to sleep.

As Trinity glanced up her gaze locked with Will's, much as it had that late-fall evening when they first met. Slow color mounted to her forehead. In the days and evenings they'd spent in the high country Will opened his heart to her about his plans for their family.

"I don't care how soon a—a little one comes along. A girl who looks just like her mother—"

"Or a little Will." Her heart thumped.

Now as Trinity held four-year-old Bruce close to her heart she knew how much their own child would mean, and what a wonderful, devoted father Will would be.

Summer continued in earnest. Trinity formed the habit of getting her work done early so she could spend long afternoons tramping the nearby woods down to the river with Bruce. His sturdy, brown legs trotted after her while she baked, sewed, cleaned, and gardened. Wise beyond his years, once she showed him the difference between weeds and vegetables, his little fingers happily pulled out the pests and he crowed with delight every time Trinity let him pull up early carrots or help her wash the leaf lettuce.

Weeks drifted into months. In August Trinity hugged a wonderful secret to her heart, savoring it alone for a few days until the right time came to share it with Will. One warm evening when they sat on the top step of the Doll House porch, her head on his shoulder, Trinity whispered, "How do you feel about having someone come live with us?" She held her breath and waited.

Will's exasperated laugh doused cold water over her. "Has Andrew been pestering you again? All I hear when I see him is how much he likes it over here and why can't he be here all the time."

The spirit of mischief marriage hadn't dimmed came fully alive in Trinity. "Oh, I'm thinking of someone younger than Andrew. Much, much younger. Even younger than Bruce."

Will held her at arm's length and his blue eyes questioned. "Who—what—why, Trinity, are we going to have a *baby*?"

Even in the laugh that followed she treasured the way he had said "we" and not just "you."

"Early, next spring."

"Yaaaaa-hooooo!" Will hugged then released her and did a dance in the yard that even surpassed the one he had done at the Indian powwow a few weeks earlier. Breathless from the wild contortions, he raced back up the steps and held her until she felt the steady beat of his strong heart.

Hours later, after the first ecstatic reaction, Will and Trinity watched the moon rise and planned for the new life God would send into their keeping.

"Trinity, about Bruce—" Will cleared his throat. "Will you feel like keeping him?"

"Why not?" She looked into his shadowed face. "I thought I could teach until the Christmas holidays. After that, I'll be home anyway." She settled her head back in the hollow of Will's shoulder where it fit so well. "I also thought I'd tell him first so he will feel our new baby is special and part his."

"You darling!" Will stroked the dark brown hair back from her forehead and kissed her temple. "I don't know why God has been so good to me in sending you into my life."

"Once I saw you, no one else mattered at all," she said softly.

"No one else really mattered to me even before I saw you," he responded. "I mean, girls or women."

Trinity smiled into the darkness. "And to think I once felt a little envious of Vi!"

"I won't be a bit surprised if Curtis and Vi make a match of it. I had that in mind when I used to drop by— that, and hoping I'd get word of Miss Schoolmarm Trinity Mason and her doings in the big city," he confessed.

"That mean Mamie said when I got married I'd gain a husband but lose a sweetheart," Trinity said, tightening her hold.

"That's what she thinks." As Will swung her up into his lap, her laugh rang over the moonlit valley and into the tall sentinel trees.

The next day Trinity sat down in the same spot on the top step and took Bruce in her lap. "How would you like to hear a special secret that no one except Will and Doc Ryan and I know?"

"Yes, yes." His eyes shone so like Will's a little pang went through Trinity.

"Many months from now, after the snow comes and goes, God is going to send a new baby to the Doll

House," she told him. "A little boy or girl that will live here with us all the time so when you go home to Daddy at night Will and I won't be so lonely."

Bruce thought about it for a moment. "Will I play with the baby when it gets big like me?"

"Of course. I'll need your help a lot since you'll be almost five years older. You'll be a cousin but I know the new baby will think you're more like a big brother."

"I never had a brother. Just Daddy and—" He wrinkled his face trying to remember. "And Mommy-who-went-to-be-with-Jesus."

How glad she felt she had told Bruce over and over about the patchwork quilt and the way dear Sarah explained her leaving him. Her arms tightened around him. "Bruce, maybe someday your daddy will find a new mommy for you and you'll have a brother or sister of your own. Will you like that?"

"Can I still be your baby's big brother?" he asked anxiously.

"We can't get along without you doing that," Trinity reassured.

"Then I think a new mommy might be nice, if I could still come here. I love you, Trin'ty."

"And I love you."

"Don't squeeze me so hard," he complained, but gave her a smile that said he really didn't mind at all. He slid down to run toward a rabbit that had curiously hopped out of a nearby bush and sat watching them with round, interested eyes.

Trinity laughed at his surprised look when the bunny disappeared before Bruce could reach him and counted her many blessings. It seemed odd that a little over a year ago she wondered if life in Cedar Ridge would stifle her. She smiled at the rebellious way she had picked up the torch thrust into her hesitant hands. If only she had known!

A wave of sheer joy washed over and through her. By Bellingham standards, she and Will had little. The hard work with few conveniences had provided a tiny home, yet that home had been furnished with *love*. The work itself brought glowing satisfaction when harvest came, but such joy paled in comparison to being cherished by a husband as Will Thatcher.

Why, she wouldn't trade places with the Queen of England with all her jewels and wealth! At this moment, Trinity Mason Thatcher was the richest woman on earth. Soon Will would bound off the crew bus bearing little resemblance to the knight in shining armor she once dreamed about—at least until he could get washed—but eager to find her waiting. He and Jamie, Trinity, and Bruce would feast on simple fare, much of it grown in her garden or from her well-stocked pantry. After Jamie and Bruce left, a late sunset promised to be spectacular and free entertainment for those who watched.

Pity the person who missed out on life as she knew it! A maple leaf drifted down from the big tree in the yard, fluttered, and lay still. Soon leaves would pack up their green for the year and don autumn coats of yellow, red and orange, russet and gold, and brown. A few months of snow and cold lay ahead, a time of white brilliance and a time for the earth to rest. Then—*spring*.

A new life, a tiny light to be fed, nurtured, and led into a steady flame for the Master.

Trinity bowed her head and thanked God.

twelve

Life took on new meaning that fall of 1919. With every stroke of ax or saw, every jar of homegrown vegetables and canned fruit labeled and stashed in the root cellar, Will and Trinity sang and laughed and loved.

The Doll House seemed to attract visitors like honeysuckle attracts insects. For those seeking sympathy and guidance, and the determination to go on and learn to prepare for whatever God had in mind for their lives, Trinity and Will were able hosts. Those who observed the love in the Doll House and wisely broke off with non-Christian sweethearts couldn't be counted.

If at times Will and Trinity felt their idyll interrupted by too many troubled persons seeking advice or just a listening ear, they smiled and made up for it when they could. Their "Doll House Ministry," as Will labeled it, left them humbled and more determined than ever to use their little home in the service of their Heavenly Father.

But storm clouds beckoned on the horizon.

Old Man Thomas, who had so eagerly bargained with Will for his rundown cabin, experienced a change of heart. Pursing his lips like a drawstring, with a greedy glint he eyed the spotless, charming Doll House and well-tended garden. All summer he'd come for his half of the produce. Now in early October his avarice overcame any scruples he might still have buried beneath his miserly grasping.

One gorgeous Saturday he reined in his horse and sidled up to the Thatchers' open front door. "Anyone home?"

"Come in, come in," Will welcomed. "Just in time for breakfast."

The visitor sniffed and his mouth watered but a single remaining shred of decency wouldn't let him break bread with them. "Naw, thanks. I just stopped by to tell you I need the place back. I 'preciate what you folks' ve done and all but with winter comin' on I can get a good price so I'm gonna sell." He cackled. "Fact is, it's already been sold. You can have 'til the first to get out."

Thunderstruck, Will stared and Trinity burst into tears. "You mean you've *sold* the Doll House? But you said— you promised—"

"There weren't no papers signed," the crafty old man said. "Don't forgit. Be out by the first." He dodged back outdoors and down the steps and hauled himself onto his horse as if pursued by devils. A long whinny and the pounding of hooves showed some uncertainty as to what he thought Will Thatcher might do if he prolonged his visit.

"It can't be true, we shook hands on it." Will's bewildered gaze sought out Trinity's confirmation. "Hardly anyone signs papers. We've always trusted everyone."

"Oh, my dear." Trinity couldn't bear the desolate look on Will's face. She ran to him and managed to smile through tears that overflowed from a breaking heart. "It's just a house." Only compassion for her tall, suffering husband kept her from wailing. All their hard work, the hours scraping and painting and building, and the shared moments alone and with family and friends rose to haunt her. A little white line came around Will's finely modeled lips and she threw her arms around him. "Please,

Will, don't look like that."

For once her entreaty went unheeded. Will remained dazed. "Honorable men don't break their word," he muttered.

With sudden insight Trinity realized that all through life Will would expect from others the total honesty and integrity by which he lived. It wouldn't be the last time he'd be disillusioned. Yet she'd rather have him as he was than a skeptic or cynic.

"It doesn't matter," she told him. "We can be thankful for the time we've had the Doll House. The real tragedy would be if we were like Old Man Thomas. Do you think he won't sometime feel guilty? Miserable at what he's done? I do." She looked into Will's face. "Besides, what's the use of worrying? Why, when Jesus comes for us we're going to be living in a mansion."

In a desperate effort to remove the stricken look from his eyes Trinity freed herself, stepped back, and lifted her skirts. As she curtsied then smiled over one shoulder she said, "Oh, yes. Do come in, everyone, and see what our Lord has already prepared."

Still inconsolable, Will turned away and ran outside. The longest hour in Trinity's life crawled by. But when Will came back, although his eyes showed the result of struggle, a half-cheery smile and look of peace were evidence of his unconquerable soul. Quietly he took the dishcloth from his wife's hands and seated her in a brightly painted chair by the matching table before sitting down across from her.

"We're going to have to decide what to do." No looking back or screaming against an unkind fate for Will Thatcher.

"I know." Trinity's shoulders slumped but she managed to straighten them.

"First thing, we need to talk with Pa."

How typical! No matter how old the Thatchers got, always the need to talk with Pa remained a vital part of their lives.

The retelling of the story kindled blue fire in Lewis Thatcher's eyes. Ruth Thatcher could not hold her tongue. "That miserable sneak! Not even the decency to warn a body." Her hands punched down bread dough as if she had Thomas pinned to the floury board.

"But where are we going to go?" Will set his lips in a straight line and crossed his arms over his chest.

How alike father and son were, Trinity noticed. One day Will would look as white-haired Lewis now did . . . and she'd love him even more, if that were possible.

Pa's anger slowly died and a gleam of excitement filled his face. "The good Lord brings good from evil, I reckon." He hooked his thumbs beneath his suspenders. "One of the neighbors asked me just the other day if I wanted to buy his forty acres next to the river. Good bottom land that needs clearing but will raise fine crops. The house is sturdy too."

"I don't know what we'd use to buy it." But Will looked excited. He knew the place well and everything Pa said about it was true.

"We can borrow at the bank. Ma and I'll cosign for you."

Trinity wanted to cry. Leave it to the Thatchers to pour the rain out of the rainbow and make things right.

"How soon could we get in? Old Man Thomas generously gave us until the first to get out of the Doll House."

Will's mouth twisted but he managed a reassuring smile for Trinity.

"If necessary you can always move in with us," Ma reminded them, her dark eyes welcoming while her hands formed bread loaves so automatically she didn't have to watch.

"I doubt that you'll need to." Pa rose and stretched. "We'll just go along and see about things now, Will. We can probably sign the papers Monday."

"This time there *will* be papers," Will flared. "Like there should have been before. I was a fool to trust Thomas."

Pa's intense gaze fixed on Will. "The way I figure, son, it's better to trust folks and sometimes have them let you down than to go through this life never trusting anyone."

"He's right." Ma smiled. "And if the milk spills, don't cry over it. Just get a mop and do something about it."

Trinity knew she'd remember Ma's advice when other hard times came. Yet on the last day of the month when she and Will closed the Doll House chapter of their life story, not even Ma's words kept back regret. For Will's sake, she didn't look back, but just tossed her head.

"Well, if you think we made this place pretty, just wait until we get in the bigger house! Your mother's already told me the neighbors are furious and to expect the biggest house-warming party ever heard of in Cedar Ridge." She linked her arm in his for the walk to their new home by the river.

Hard work lay ahead, not so much in the house but outside. Only a portion of the forty acres had been cleared for crops and Will and Pa spent every spare moment cutting timber to be sold for cash, burning out stumps, and turning the land into rich fields ready for spring planting.

Trinity's schedule proved as busy. Between teaching, cooking, cleaning, and fixing up her house December crept up on her, a time of occasional snow but unseasonably warm. Will rejoiced. The longer a real freeze held off, the easier to till the ground.

"I think you're working too hard," he told Trinity one night. His keen eyes saw the tired droop of her lips when she didn't realize he was watching her.

"I'm all right." Yet pale blue shadows lay under her eyes.

"Are you sure? Maybe you should see Doc Ryan again."

She laughed and a warm flush erased signs of weariness. "He has enough to do without my bothering him." She yawned. "Nothing like fresh air and a good supper to make a person sleepy." She yawned again, and stretched like a lazy cat. "Will, on our honeymoon, you said someday you'd quote some other poetry. Besides 'Betty and the Bear.' "

He left his chair and came to the couch where she'd curled up after supper.

"Good old William Wordsworth said it all." He began softly and tenderly. " 'She was a phantom of delight when first she gleamed upon my sight.' " Before Trinity could reply he smiled. "Since we've been married I appreciate some things that come later in the poem. 'A creature not too bright or good for human nature's daily food.' " He took her hand in both of his. "The last lines are the best. 'A perfect woman, nobly planned to warn, to comfort and command; And yet a spirit still, and bright with something of angelic light.' "

Trinity's heart jumped the same way it had when she first saw Will coming down the stairs more than a year before. How wrong Mamie had been! Will remained her sweetheart as well as her husband. A little prayer winged upward from her overflowing heart.

Although she loved teaching at the White Rock School, Trinity rejoiced when the Christmas holidays came. Will had not been the first to notice she looked tired; she had felt that way for some time. Maybe Will was right: The next time they went into town she *would* go see Doc. Probably all she needed was a tonic.

That same night snow came like fleece. All night it silently covered the countryside, softening the naked fields exposed by Will's clearing, and adding jaunty caps to the fenceposts. When the moon finally peeked out to illumine the transformed mountains and valley, more than a foot of fluff clung to the ground.

"How beautiful!" Trinity flung open the front door, heedless of the cold air rushing in. Red spots of excitement colored her cheeks and her eyes danced. When Will protested and closed the door, she washed his face with the handful of white she'd snatched from outside the door.

"Just for that you have to make biscuits for breakfast," he ordered in his best lord-of-the-manor voice then followed her to the kitchen, cut bacon from a big slab, and brought in an enormous pile of wood. "Looks like it may snow again. We might as well be prepared." He grinned and stamped out. "I'll milk the cow and see if there are any eggs."

Trinity sang while she worked. Being snowed in could be fun and give her time to talk with Will. So often they were both tired by the time evening came. Today would be different. She busily planned meals in her mind, simple ones that would cook themselves and leave her free.

For three days it snowed most of the time, sometimes twenty-four inches in twenty-four hours. Will quoted John Greenleaf Whittier's "Snowbound" in his most dramatic style and Trinity marveled again at how a young boy's determination to learn had committed to memory far more than many college professors she knew!

"I'll never forget these three days," Trinity confessed on Christmas Eve afternoon. "I love having our families come—and Bruce—but for once it's nice just to have you." She patted her hair smooth and reached for a warm cap. Although the snow had ceased and the benevolent moon turned the valley to silver, a cold snap crisped the air.

"Will you be warm enough?" Will asked. A little frown crossed his forehead. "I should have gone over earlier and borrowed Pa's car so we wouldn't have to walk. The snow's crusty enough to hold us but it won't hold the horses." He frowned again. "It isn't too late and I know Pa's broken out the lane to the main road."

"For that little way?" Trinity teased. "I'm neither sugar nor salt. Then again, I'm so bundled up I just might melt from all the layers of clothes!" She pulled the bright stocking cap over her hair and buttoned her warm coat clear to her chin.

Ten minutes later as she stood in the crystal night she

whispered, "I wouldn't have missed this for anything."
She clutched Will's mittened hand with her own and
gazing skyward drew in a deep breath. "Can even heaven
be more beautiful?"

Will silently shook his head. White-clad trees dripped
long, gleaming icicles. Diamond dust sparkled in the
moonlight. The howl of a distant wolf and the cry of a
lone eagle drifted in the pure air, a psalm of praise to
their Creator.

They stood until Trinity shivered in spite of her warm
clothing, as much from the night splendor as the cold.
Will wrapped his arms around her and held his cold
cheek next to hers. In a husky voice he said, "We'd better
go, you mustn't get chilled."

She turned a reluctant glance at the shimmering night
and trotted with him down the cleared lane to the big,
noisy house that spilled over with lamplight and
laughter.

All evening in the midst of the gaiety Trinity thought
of the rare beauty they had been privileged to see. She
laughed and ate and exclaimed over the many gifts from
the family, secretly proud of the hours she'd spent
embroidering pillow cases and making rag dolls and
toys for the others. *Here she belonged.*

Later as Trinity and Will walked home neither could
have foreseen the dangers of such an exquisite winter
night. As they walked close to the river, the mischievous
spirit Trinity had never lost made her break free of Will's
protective arm and whirl in a circle in front of him. "Isn't
this wonderful?"

"Trinity, be careful!"

His warning cry came too late.

Trinity's right foot slipped on an icy patch. A pulse beat later she fell hard and skidded toward the sluggish water.

"*Trinity!*" Will leaped for her with incredible speed. He grabbed her coat sleeve and yanked, but not before she'd broken the thin ice and plunged waist-deep into the freezing water.

Will snatched off his heavy coat and bundled it around her legs, caught her in his arms, and staggered toward home in one swift motion. By the time he got her inside their own warm home, Trinity's teeth chattered like hail on a milk can.

"I–I–I'm all r–r–right," she tried to tell him but she couldn't stop shaking. Even a rubdown in front of the glowing fire, her warmest robe, and a steaming mug of hot chocolate did little to melt the cold core inside her.

"It's to bed with you." Will scooped her up and tucked her in. For hours she lay close to him, firmly putting from her mind the terrible fear that attacked when she felt herself sliding into the river. Gradually the shivers stopped and she slept, only to awaken burning hot. "Hot, so hot." Why couldn't she speak clearly? Her tongue felt thick and fuzzy. She flung off the quilts and half sat up.

In an instant Will had her in his arms. "What is it?"

"I'm so hot." She raised one hand to her forehead and licked parched lips.

"You're burning up." Will gently pushed her back on the pillow, then went to the kitchen for a tall glass of ice-cold water.

Trinity eagerly snatched the glass and drained it. "More."

He refilled her glass then brought a basin and soft

cloth. He washed her face and hands. "Feel better?"

"Yes." Then why did she feel so dizzy the room whirled? "Will, I think I'm sick."

"Are you in any pain?" His sharp question cut through her semiconscious state.

"No, just tired." She closed her eyes.

"Trinity, I'm going for Ma. I won't be long. Don't get out of bed."

She camouflaged a sob with a croaky laugh. A door opened then closed. She didn't care. Had the house caught fire? She fought the quilts and gave up, too tired to push them away. "God, are You here? I'm so hot. The baby . . . ."

Jumbled sights and sounds haunted her. Will's voice saying something about a river. Periods of shivering followed by burning up. Something pressing on her chest. Why, where did Doc Ryan come from? Was someone sick?

"Pneumonia." She caught the word then whirled down into a void broken at last by excruciating pain. "Will, help me! God, are You here?"

Something stung her arm. A pungent, smothering cloth fell over her nose . . . then, nothing.

thirteen

The strands of sleep that had clouded Trinity's mind one by one drifted away. At last she opened her eyes. She must be late. Why hadn't Will called her? She'd never arrived late to school, even when she was a child. She struggled up and tried to swing her feet out of bed.

"No, Trinity." Will came in from the kitchen, haggard and thinner than she'd ever seen him. He quickly covered her again and sat on the edge of their bed.

"Don't talk," he told her. "You've been very sick but now you're better. Rest, and I'll bring you some broth a little later."

It was enough—for then.

When Trinity woke a few hours later with a clearer mind she lay still, trying to piece together what had happened. Never before had she felt so weak, so like a newborn calf trying to stand on wobbly legs.

Newborn. Panic gripped her. She laid one hand on her flat stomach. Please, God, let me find this is a nightmare, she pleaded and blinked hard.

"*Will*!" She screamed, and sat up, ignoring the weakness that threatened to claim her again with greedy fingers.

"I'm here." He came to the bed in long strides and took her in his arms.

"The baby, little Will, I—"

"Trinity." His steady grasp on her shoulders kept her from falling. "You've had pneumonia. We all thought we'd lose you." Unchecked tears flowed in furrows down his gaunt face.

"But little Will," she protested, knowing in her heart what she had to hear but unwilling and unable to believe it.

Will's grip tightened. Trinity could see her disheveled self reflected in his eyes. He took a long, unsteady breath.

"He didn't make it, my darling."

She sagged against him. How could life be so punishing? Didn't God love her anymore? What had she done to deserve this? Through her churning thoughts came the invading, terrible truth. "It's my fault." She tore free of Will's arms. "In the woods. I shouldn't have—"

"Listen to me, Trinity Thatcher!" Something in Will's face and his fierce voice stilled her torment. "Have I ever lied to you?"

Surprise jerked her head into a shake.

"Do you believe I ever will?"

"N–no." Why didn't he just go and leave her alone?

Will's eyes blazed and he forced her chin up until she had to look into his face. "Little Will couldn't have lived anyway." The muscles of his strong throat contracted. "Doc Ryan discovered first off when he examined you that the little guy's heart had something wrong with it. Even if he had made it the full time, Doc says he wasn't strong enough to live. Nothing you did changed things except we thought we'd lose both of you."

"Wh–where is he?" The words almost stuck in her throat.

Will's face grayed and he nodded toward the window. To Trinity's amazement the snow had gone. "Out there, beneath the cottonwood."

"Why, how long have I been sick?" Trinity demanded. "I want to hold my baby." She slumped and Will let her down.

"We couldn't wait. We buried him a week ago. You were too sick to—" Will's lips set then he forced a smile. "We gave little Will back to God on Christmas, the same day He sent His Son. It's a new year now, Trinity. God willing, a better one."

Long after he slipped out to do a few chores Trinity lay still. Her empty arms ached for the too-small baby Will had told her about. Dry-eyed, she wondered how she could live. A passionate wave of protest born of sickness and nurtured by loss welled up inside her. "Oh, God, how could You let this happen?" Did she shout or whisper? What difference did it make? Where had God been when she needed Him so much? Why had He forsaken her?

She closed her eyes, willing away the agony. For her husband's sake she must be strong. Could even God help her do this?

Will quietly opened the back door and crossed to the bedroom. "Trinity?"

"Shh." She raised her thin, white hand. "Listen!"

Like a melody from the past, glorious strains of music reached Will's ears. Months vanished. Once again he stood in Ma's doorway, transfixed by an indescribable song. Now it sounded familiar. Swelling, dying, rising again to triumph, it brought healing, even as it had done when Daniel died.

When the last note faded Trinity held out her hands to him. "We can go on." Every trace of bitterness had fled with the music.

"It's what Ma and I heard after we lost Daniel," Will said. He stumbled to the bedside and buried his face in Trinity's lap. Great sobs shook him. All she could do was stroke the thick, waving, golden-brown hair until he stilled. It might be weeks, months, or even years before they could talk about this moment but another strong link in the chains that bound them had been forged by their loss.

Within a few weeks Trinity had regained much of her strength. Yet a little dread filled her. In spite of the comfort received through God's loving mercy, she didn't know how she could face Bruce when he came back to her.

The first time, she couldn't speak. She opened her arms wide and he climbed into them. They rocked silently for a long while before the little boy said, "Daddy told me little Will went to live with Mama and Jesus."

Trinity's arms tightened. "Yes." Warm tears splashed onto Bruce's hand.

"Daddy said heaven's better than here." Bruce wiggled until he could look directly into her eyes. The same blueness that characterized his father and Will demanded her full attention. "He said little Will wasn't strong like me and if he'd got borned I couldn't play with him when he got big." He hesitated.

"Trin'ty, is Daddy right? Is little Will all better now and does he love Mommy like I love you? Is he happy? Is Jesus glad Mommy and little Will's with Him and God?"

"Of course." Just saying it brought back all Trinity's

hope for eternal life.

Bruce wiped away her tears with a grubby little hand. "Then why are you crying?" He anxiously peered into her face, seeking reassurance.

This time the rush of tears healed instead of hurt. Trinity hugged the perceptive little boy who in his own childish way had gone straight to the heart of what life was about. "Sometimes people cry when they're happy and sometimes when they're sad, Bruce. I miss little Will and so does his father, but I'm glad he's well and happy." She took a long, unsteady breath.

"So am I," a voice said.

How long had Will stood in the doorway listening? Trinity wondered.

Bruce slid from her lap and ran to his beloved Will. "Do you cry 'cause you miss little Will?" he demanded.

The tall man caught the little boy up in his strong arms. "Sometimes." Trinity swallowed hard but Bruce hadn't finished. From the shelter of the welcoming hug he looked at Trinity, then back at Will. He patted Will's face and said, "Don't cry, Will. You've still got me. And Trin'ty."

Will pulled him close and his gaze met Trinity's across the loving child's shoulder. "Yes, I do, Bruce, and I thank God."

So did Trinity.

A few weeks later Pa Thatcher crossed the January fields to Will and Trinity's home. "Well, that's good," he said after shrugging out of his coat and seeing the roaring fire in the fireplace. He held his workworn hands to the welcome blaze. " 'Pears to me you folks've made this place every bit as cozy as the Doll House."

Trinity looked around in satisfaction. The perky red tiebacks she'd finished just this morning and fastened around the white curtains matched the bright red of their table and chairs. She laughed. "Every time we want to change colors we just paint our chairs and table and find matching strips to tie back the curtains."

"Yellow first, now red. We still have blue and green and orange and purple—"

"*Purple*!" Trinity swung toward Will in protest. "No purple chairs and table for us. They'd give us indigestion."

"I reckon they might at that," Pa agreed, and his eyes twinkled.

"I don't suppose you walked over tonight just to admire our red table and chairs, now did you, Pa?" Will lounged back in his chair and grinned.

"Well, no." Pa's twinkle faded and he cleared his throat. "I—we—the School Board—" He shot a quick glance at Trinity. "The teacher we got to take your place since you were sick and all isn't working out. Come to find out, the city slicker's letting the big boys get away with all kinds of mischief when they should be learning their lessons. T'other day I drove past and you know what I saw?"

His face turned red with indignation. "There was the teacher chasing around and around White Rock School after one of the boys, and the rest of the school, even the little ones, chased around right behind her like the tail of a kite! I called a special board meeting right away and—" His eyes gleamed. "Let's just say that by mutual agreement we now need a teacher."

Trinity's fingers tightened in her lap. "You need *me*?"

"We sure do." Pa's hearty endorsement ended with a frown. "Now if you feel you can't, we'll understand, but meanwhile our young folks aren't being taught."

"You don't have to go back if you don't want to, Trinity."

She caught Will's anxious glance and thought for a moment. Just this afternoon when she put the last stitches in the tiebacks she'd wondered what to do next. Once her energy returned after her sickness and the loss of little Will, she found herself filling the hours with hard, healing work. Until spring came and she could get out in the garden the barren hours could only bring back the lurking sadness.

"I can start Monday morning," she told Pa and his big smile showed pride in her as well as relief. "I'm sorry my pupils have changed so much in such a short time but I won't take sauciness."

"You don't have to. The troublemakers have been warned that one complaint and they're out."

Trinity felt troubled. "I hope that never happens." In the remaining days she went over her meager wardrobe and prayed for wisdom—and strength—in the new situation.

The new schoolmarm, as Will persisted in calling her, found the boys who had come since Christmas gave her no trouble. Will's own brother Andrew was one of the eighth graders she'd be expected to prepare well enough to put through the state exams. Would the fun-loving boy take advantage of how well he knew her and the hours they'd enjoyed together at the Doll House? She couldn't help asking Will about it.

"Ha! Pa told Andrew he'd be in real trouble if he got out of line. Besides, he thinks too much of you to be a nuisance."

Will's prophecy came true. Not only did Andrew call her Mrs. Thatcher as respectfully as if she hadn't been Trinity to him for months, he excelled in his studies, especially mathematics. A few weeks after Trinity began teaching the White Rock pupils, a group of neighbors came to school one morning with a problem.

"We have a piece of land that needs splitting up," one of them said scratching his head. "Now it has a creek and trees and—" He went on to explain all the factors. "We just can't figger how to cut it in pieces and be fair to everyone." He smiled at Trinity. "Most of us didn't have the chance to get past third or fourth grade. D'you s'pose some of your class can help us out? We're offering a brand-new twenty-dollar bill to whoever solves the problem." His grin broadened. "Mayhap it'll have to be you, teacher."

"Oh, I'd like our class to try first," she told him. The older pupils' eyes shone at the mention of twenty dollars. What couldn't they buy with it!

"Now what we need's a dee-tailed written-out way to split up the parcel of land," the spokesman said. "This is what we've got." He took a piece of chalk and drew a rude sketch outlining the land and its features on the blackboard behind Trinity's desk. "Remember, it has to be fair to all four of us." He dusted his hands off on his overalls. "When can we get an answer?"

"Today's Monday. Give us until Friday." Trinity shook hands with each of the visitors and then turned to her class. "How exciting! I hope many of you will try to earn the prize. Copy the picture to take home and good luck."

Tuesday morning Andrew Thatcher burst into the one-room school waving a piece of paper. "I've got it, Mrs. Thatcher. I mean, I have it," he quickly corrected himself. His dark eyes inherited from his mother sparkled and his white teeth shone.

"So soon? Oh, Andrew, I'm afraid you worked too fast."

He shook his head emphatically. "Look, each of the families should have some trees and access to the creek and a field. See how I did it?"

Trinity gasped. With painstaking care, the tall boy had accurately pinpointed the only way the property could be divided without sacrificing one thing in favor of another. "Good for you," she burst out. "I believe that twenty-dollar bill is already yours."

"I hate to wait 'til Friday," Andrew admitted, and sat down behind his desk to wait for the rest of the pupils to arrive.

"So do I." Trinity laughed with her star mathematics student.

She had barely rung the bell on Friday morning before the four men returned. "I hear tell by the grapevine we've got ourselves a winner," their leader announced. He and the other men gathered around Trinity's desk and looked over the many suggestions given, sometimes nodding but always going on.

Andrew's solution, written clearly and in simple, explanatory language, came last. The minute the men saw it a grunt of approval told the waiting class the verdict.

"Now why didn't *we* think of that?" One strong farmer

shook his head.

" 'Cause we ain't eddicated," another said.

Trinity caught the wistfulness in his voice. "There are many kinds of education, gentlemen. You know crops and weather and the land better than most who have heads stuffed with book knowledge." She noticed the involuntary straightening of shoulders bent with honest toil. She continued, "You also understand God's creation and His loving care. You've taught your children the really important things in life. I just give them new ways to help solve old problems."

"And we're thankful for that," the spokesman said.

Trinity felt choked up and the wave of applause from her students only ended when the farmer raised one hand.

"Andy Thatcher, we're beholden to you." He carefully folded the paper and tucked it in his pocket. With his other hand he took out the promised twenty-dollar bill and gave it to the excited boy. "You keep right on listenin' to your teacher and your ma and pa and you'll be all right."

Each of the grateful men shook hands first with Andrew, then with Trinity, and left. While the class settled down Trinity asked, "What are you going to do with your money, Andrew?"

His whole face lit up. "Pa needs a new plow but he says he won't take my money, so I'm going to get a horse. Curtis promised if I won the prize he'd give me enough more to get a first-rate horse. It won't be as good as Will's Bullet but it will be all mine. I may even get a colt or a filly and raise it myself."

Trinity congratulated him again and got busy with her

lessons. In a considerate gesture, she didn't call Andrew to attention when she caught him gazing out the window. Her spirit empathized with his—already free and racing with the wind, hair flying along with his horse's mane and tail. A surge of longing for spring left her shaken.

But February continued to bring more snowstorms and Will even had to break trail for Trinity to get to school. One night she awakened to a strange whining sound and an unusual smell in the air. She reached out for Will, but the place beside her was empty.

"Will?"

"Here, Trinity," he called from the window.

"What is it?"

"The Chinook wind. Tomorrow the snow will be gone. Feel how warm it is?"

Barefoot, she padded to his side and looked out. Branches swayed against the side of the house and warm, moist air billowed the curtains at the open window. She breathed deeply. How could she have forgotten the Chinook wind, a true harbinger of spring in the Northwest?

All night the Chinook continued and when morning came only stray patches of snow remained, mostly under the shelter of tall trees.

Now a new roaring had replaced the gentle whine. While Trinity dressed and started making breakfast, the sound filled her ears.

"Trinity, come see." Will dashed into the house, full milk pails in each hand. He set them on the counter, grabbed her arm, and hurried her outdoors across the plowed garden spot toward the increasing roar.

They stepped out from trees that hid the view and Trinity stopped short. "My word!"

Where had the friendly river gone, the stream in which she'd often waded? Worse, where had this greedy, sucking brown monster come from, roiling, tossing, bearing mighty downed logs as if they were chips? Jolted by the terrible but compelling sight, she could do nothing but stand and gaze. She had seen what happened when a Chinook wind brought the snow from the encircling hills too fast. Humans in all their wisdom could not control the elements and Trinity shivered and stared at the face of flood.

"I just hope it doesn't get much higher," Will said in her ear.

"Why? You don't mean . . . ." Her voice failed her.

Will's far-seeing eyes and pointing finger stopped her heart. "It's already crept up a foot since we got here. Most of the big log jam is gone." Worry filled his stern face.

Trinity clutched his arm for support and riveted her gaze at the encroaching danger. "It won't take our place. It can't, can it?" she pleaded.

"I pray to God it won't but I've never seen the Cedar so high," he admitted between tightened lips. "We'd better get back and be prepared, just in case."

With a final look at the menacing waters, Trinity stumbled after him back toward their home, too stunned even to pray for deliverance.

fourteen

Will checked the rising water every hour, yet every time he came in he had to report it was higher. By noon he no longer needed to tell her: The river had cut to the edge of their garden-to-be and Trinity could see its gleam from the window.

Trinity frantically gathered clothing and dishes, anything she could quickly pack in case they were forced to flee. She prayed as she worked. "God, please make the waters recede. We've worked so hard after losing the Doll House—and little Will." Her lips trembled and she refused to look out again, even though the *lap, lap* sound came from the sheet of water that had already reached the barn. She knew the cow was safe, and Will's horse. He'd taken them earlier to the far end of the forty acres. No flood except the one in the time of Noah could reach them there.

Her will power caved in when she heard a crash. She flew to the door and looked out. Empty wooden boxes they'd stacked behind the barn floated like miniature arks. A gray squirrel scolded, rode one until it beached against a fir, and scurried to safety in the top branches.

Will looked ten years older when he splashed back to the porch. Trinity saw how he measured the scant ten feet between the creeping waters and where they stood.

"If it comes five feet closer, we leave. Have you got things ready? Pa's on his way with the car."

"Yes, all I could. I stacked the chairs on top of the table in case water and mud come in the house and took up the

162

rugs in the bedroom." She tried to smile and knew how weak it must look. "If it isn't Old Man Thomas, it's something else."

"We still have each other—and God, no matter what happens."

"I know." She put her arms around him, feeling ashamed. For a moment she closed her eyes against the relentless flood. When she opened them, she blinked twice. "Will, I think it's receding!"

He tore free of her grasp and whirled. Joy lit up his face. "You're right, thank God!" Arms around each other they watched the Cedar River move back inch by inch, as if angry at being cheated of its prey. Although the ground remained sodden, by night Trinity could no longer see the water. She thanked God again.

March stormed its way in and out; April bloomed and so did Trinity. If what she suspected were true, soon she'd have wonderful news for Will but she must wait a few weeks to make sure.

Doc Ryan confirmed her suspicions and in late May Trinity cooked a special supper on a Saturday night. Jamie and Bruce still ate with them Mondays through Fridays and, dear as they were, her news must first be shared with Will.

"Do you know you get prettier all the time?" Will asked when after supper they walked the greening fields, already showing signs of early garden produce planted after the flood.

"Do I? I'm glad you think so." Trinity breathed in the fresh April air and led him to a downed tree stump. "Will, something good has come from all our sadness. We're going to have a child."

Will looked at her and then did an Irish jig in the clearing. A passing night hawk paused in flight, and seemed to cry out congratulations.

"When?"

"Probably early January."

Will lifted and whirled her and then held her a little way off from him. "God is good." His tender smile curled into her heart and warmed it.

A little later she tremulously asked, "Do you want a boy?" She saw the quick flash of pain before he whispered, "I don't care. Just as long as our baby's healthy."

Time seemed to fly after Trinity finished out the school term, and spent a happy, dreaming summer working with Will as much as he allowed and sewing garments for the new spark growing within her. She often thought of the tiny soul that had come and gone without her ever seeing him, but she rejoiced knowing that, through God's love, someday they would be reunited. Now a new child must claim her attention.

"Will, I'd like to name our baby Candace if it's a girl," she said one day in early fall. "I looked it up in that old book Vi still has and Candace means 'glittering' or 'flowing white.'" She bent her head. "But I want to call her Candleshine, just in the family."

"Suits me." Will looked puzzled, however, and Trinity tried to explain.

"I keep feeling God and my ancestors who served Him expect me to hold high the torch they've passed to me." She let her hands rest in her lap. "Sometimes my torch isn't very bright and I wonder if it's gone out. Then, like the flame of the smallest candle, it keeps burning but it needs to be carefully tended. Today while I was reading my Bible I found a verse I'd never seen before, or at least I don't remember it."

Trinity reached into the modest V-neck of her printed gown and withdrew a small paper tucked just above her heart.

" '*For thou wilt light my candle; the Lord my God will enlighten my darkness.*' " She refolded the paper and replaced it in her dress. "It's Psalm 18:28 and it's almost like David wrote it for me." Her long lashes sparkled in the firelight. "I know without God I—we could never have made it through the last year."

"Candleshine she shall be. If it's a boy, how about Daniel Edmund?"

"Doesn't Pa want us to use his name?" Trinity asked.

Will shook his head. "I already mentioned it but Pa said he'd rather we used Daniel. What does that mean, anyway?"

Wrinkling her forehead to remember, Trinity finally said, "It means 'God is my judge.' "

"Good enough." Will stretched and yawned. "Well, Mrs. Thatcher, five o'clock comes mighty early. Let's go to bed."

Thanksgiving came and went, a time of harvest and praising God. Christmas neared, not white and frozen like the year before but rainy and gray. Yet no gray existed in Will and Trinity's world. Doc Ryan pronounced her in excellent health and the baby's heartbeat sound and strong.

Before Christmas Trinity awakened in the night and for a moment she felt the past year had been a dream. Pain clutched at her as it had then.

"Will, I'm really sick."

"The baby? It's too early, isn't it?"

"Yes, you know I'm not due until January." A spasm caught her and she gripped his strong arm. "Go get your mother. I don't think I can hold off until Doc comes."

Will leaped into his clothes and tore out the door. Again Trinity heard the sound of racing hooves. She fought fear that attacked even sooner than the premature pains. "God, don't let it be like before!"

Incredibly, Ruth Thatcher appeared by the bed, her clothing askew but the certainty of her own skill plain on her face. In quiet tones she told Will what to do and encouraged Trinity. "So what if the baby's early? Maybe you didn't figure right. Or perhaps the little one's tired of doing nothing but sleeping." Her soothing flow relaxed the struggling girl and in less than an hour a lusty yell told Trinity everything was all right.

"A girl! Candace or Candleshine," Will whispered. Ma quickly cleaned and wrapped the baby while Will mopped Trinity's hot face. Bathed, powdered, and in a clean gown and freshly made bed, Trinity held her tiny, perfect girl. A final wail broke off sharply and, minutes later, the newest Thatcher fell asleep, filled and content.

Doc Ryan arrived a few hours later and his beaming face resembled nothing more than the rising sun. "Don't know why you called me," he grumbled in mock disgust. "Ruth Thatcher's as good as a doctor any day. Sorry your own ma couldn't be here, though. She's another dandy when it comes to bringing babies."

Trinity smiled at Mama who had ridden out with the doctor. "She's staying for a few days until I can care for our baby."

Mama's slow smile showed the new bond between

them. More than mother and daughter, the two women now shared an interest in the blanketed bundle at Trinity's breast.

A few days later when Will had gone to work and Candace lay asleep in the handmade cradle Pa had once fashioned for little Will, Mercy Mason was alone with Trinity. "Trinity, there's something I have to say to you."

It had been years since she used that no-nonsense tone of voice to her grown daughter. Trinity couldn't imagine what Mama had in mind.

"It's about Candleshine." Already the family had begun to use the nickname instead of the more formal Candace. "Now, I know how hard it is to lose a baby." Her face shadowed and Trinity remembered the little one that came after Albert and before Robert William. "The hardest thing I've found in raising Rob is in not trying to smother him."

A rush of understanding came to Trinity. "You mean, once you've lost one, it's natural to be too protective?"

"Yes," Mama sighed, "it isn't good for mother or child to have so much concern neither one can grow." Her smile brightened the whole room. "Enough said. Now, what did you want me to get ready for supper?"

Long after Mama went back to tend her own happy, noisy family, Trinity thought about what she'd said. It made sense. But had the warning come in time? Already Trinity had held her breath and checked on Candleshine again and again just to make sure she was all right. Will laughingly threatened to kidnap Candleshine and bundle her off to his parents so his wife could get some rest.

"Lord," she suddenly prayed. "This is Your child, the candle You lit and sent to shine in our lives. Forgive me for my fears. Help me trust You. I give this child's life to You. In Jesus' name, Amen."

Trinity never forgot either the prayer or the promise she made on that winter day. Every time Candace coughed or cried, the young mother reminded herself that God controlled the beautiful child. In time, it became such a habit that even when real danger threatened, she could rely on the ingrained faith won by persistence and prayer.

The baby grew like rushes in a swamp. At a year old, she toddled after six-year-old Bruce the way a caboose chases a long train. "Big Brother Bruce" loved his tiny cousin even more than he loved going to school. From his first glimpse to make sure the new baby really *was* all right, he hung on the crib, talked to the child, and adored her. Even when his father Jamie married a kind-hearted neighbor woman whose heart proved big enough to accept both Jamie and his son without question, Bruce spent as much time with Trinity and Candleshine as possible. His new stepmother Charity didn't have an envious bone in her body and openly rejoiced at the unusual bond that existed between Bruce and the other Thatchers.

Sometimes when no one could hear, Trinity sighed. No more babies had come and Doc Ryan said he suspected none would. *If only she could have given Will a son*! Yet he worshiped his daughter next to God and his wife. Jamie graciously consented to Bruce tagging Will, and the tall man, stripling boy, and tiny girl became a familiar sight. Often Trinity accompanied them on tramps, but even when she had inside chores, pride lifted the corners of her mouth.

One late afternoon she dropped to a chair on the porch and took stock. She thought of gentle Faith, now happily married and living within riding distance. Donald McKenna had proved to be the fine man Trinity recognized so long ago and a baby would be arriving soon to complete their household.

Hope and her John remained in Panama. The trip Hope promised long ago had been delayed by the birth of a daughter—also named Hope—but the past summer the three had finally come home. What a glorious reunion!

Edmund found a special Christian girl and had recently purchased a small home in Cedar Ridge.

Albert liked school, the outdoors, and trains, hoping someday to "drive a ying-yanger." When he wasn't busy with studies and chores and playing ball, he spent every free minute with the engineers and firemen asking all sorts of questions.

Rob continued healthy, but Grandma Clarissa did not. Every time she saw her little grandmother Trinity felt happy and sad at the same time. Grandma Clarissa had prepared to meet her God. The radiance of her thin face and wrinkled cheeks showed more clearly than words her longing to answer God's call when it came time to be with her husband.

Once Trinity found Grandma Clarissa alone in the twilight. She took the worn hand and impulsively asked, "Grandma, if you could live life all over again, what would you want changed or do differently?"

A final ray of sun gleamed in the soft, white hair, lingered on the wise eyes, and highlighted a face at peace.

For a long moment Grandma didn't answer. Then she

patted Trinity's hand with her free one. "Why, child, how could I ask for things to be different when our Heavenly Father has walked with me every day of my life?"

She leaned her head back on the crocheted chair cover and gazed into the sky. "Many times I cried out for answers when trouble came. Sometimes I forgot to thank our Lord for His mercy. Yes, I would have changed things to suit myself, especially when your grandfather died." Her lips trembled and Trinity thought she looked like a young girl.

"You still miss him, don't you?"

Clarissa squeezed her granddaughter's hand. "Every day since he went ahead the way he used to do when we walked brushy trails and he cleared the path for me to follow." Her unsteady voice told its own story.

"Child, it's the hard times that bring you together— and the little things. You told me once that one of the greatest gifts Will ever gave you was when he built a sleeping porch on your home." She smiled at Trinity again. "You've learned the secret of real happiness. It's in sharing whatever life offers and going on when you aren't sure you can."

"Ma Thatcher says instead of crying over spilled milk we have to get a mop and do something about it," Trinity said.

"She's right." The frail little woman sat up straight and strength seemed to flow from her to Trinity. "A body who sits around and moans too long about things that can't be changed is a disgrace to God."

"*Grandma!*" Trinity had never heard such a statement from her gentle grandmother.

"It's true. We're supposed to have faith. How do you think God feels when we snivel and complain instead of hanging onto His coattails for dear life until He makes things better?"

Trinity tucked away the startling piece of advice in her workbox of memories. When needed, she would examine and test it for herself. "Grandma, will I ever be as good as you?"

"Land sakes, Trinity, if you don't make a heap better job of living than I've done, what will happen to that torch I passed down? It's up to every generation to raise truth higher and brighter . . . for the times ahead will be dark, as dark as that."

She pointed into the blackness that had fallen and Trinity shivered at the certainty in her grandmother's voice.

fifteen

The first of Grandma Clarissa's "black times" arrived late in 1929. Caught up in the changing seasons, and watching Bruce and baby Candleshine grow, the Thatchers and Masons paid little heed to the larger world except to shake their heads at the painted flappers and news of gangsters, bootleg whiskey, and speakeasies. More interest lay with the wave of revival meetings sweeping the country. Billy Sunday, a baseball player turned evangelist, became the most popular religious leader of the time. Some said during his ministry he preached to over 100 million and saw over a million converted to Christ!

Grandma Clarissa died when Candleshine was still small, but her excitement over going on lessened the sadness of those left behind. Her passing seemed to increase their determination to live for Jesus and join her someday.

Fourteen-year-old Bruce and nine-year-old Candleshine surprisingly kept their special friendship. Trinity sometimes despaired of her daughter ever being anything but a tomboy. Time after time she answered a cheerful call and found Candleshine nonchalantly hanging upside down from a sturdy tree branch, or with Bruce playing marbles. After a battle royal before Candleshine entered first grade, already reading and eager to learn more, Trinity accepted the inevitable. Later she would laugh about it, but the day Candleshine made her own little declaration of independence was *not* funny.

Grandma Mercy loved the flaxen-haired little girl and was loved in return, but not enough for Candleshine to suffer the indignity of having her hair fixed in long curls for school.

"I don't like curls," she told her grandmother and shook her head. "They get in the way when I play."

"You look lovely," said Grandma finishing her handi-work with a huge blue bow.

A half-hour later when the house felt too quiet Trinity looked around for Candleshine. She finally found her — huddled in the warm triangle made by the kitchen wood range, scissors in hand. A pile of shining curls lay scattered over her lap and the floor.

"Candleshine, what a naughty thing to do!" Trinity exclaimed.

Unrepentant, her five year old muttered, "I don't like curls."

The next morning all Trinity could do with the jagged hair was pull it back into two skimpy pigtails so tight Candleshine felt her eyes slant. Never again did her mother or grandmother put curls in the fair hair.

When Wall Street crashed and the world panicked, Will and Trinity wondered how it would affect them and those they loved. Before long, they found out. Many of their friends and neighbors who depended on now-closed banks lost everything, took what they could get, and moved away in search of nonexistent work. Trinity's heart ached and the dread she'd felt years before when her grandmother predicted hard and dark times almost overwhelmed her. Only her faith in God and love for her family kept her going.

Months passed. Will took on every job he could find but times got even worse. Now Trinity's early training served her well. Will's worn coats and pants became treasures to cut down and sew into clothing for Candleshine. Along with floursacks bleached for under-clothes and knitted mittens, Trinity's knack with fancy stitches added flair to the garments. Yet even her talents couldn't stop the juggernaut of poverty rolling over the land. Trinity shared her distress in a letter to Hope.

Although I have time, I can't mail this letter right away. Frankly, my dear sister, I have neither a postage stamp nor the money to buy one. At least we have plenty to eat from our garden. Our cows and chickens supply us well and Will killed a deer not long ago. He brings in fish once in a while when he has time.

Yet we are wondrously happy. Candleshine is long-legged, knobby-kneed, and sweet-tempered. I just pray for all those who have so much less, the ones who fight over garbage in the cities.

We try to help where we can. Will has told many of the townspeople who are down and out they can come help themselves to our garden surplus. But Hope, can you believe only one family came? The others complained and asked why Will couldn't load up the produce and deliver it to their doors!

He replied that he's working day and night for his own family and if they're too blasted lazy to walk or ride out and get food they'll just have to do without. I don't blame him.

There was more, but Trinity had to hold her letter for over a week until Will brought home a little cash earned by hauling wood.

Trinity scrupulously kept track of every penny he earned. Ironically, now when they needed money so badly, the teaching doors had closed for her. School boards told her pointblank they regretted it but jobs must go to men who had families to feed. She could understand, even while wondering what would become of them. During the worst year of all, Trinity discovered on the last day of December Will's earnings for twelve-hour days, not counting the farm chores she and Candleshine couldn't handle, amounted to only fifty-dollars. Fifty dollars—to stretch for things they couldn't raise or do without! To make matters worse, Edmund Mason fell ill and died. Mercy Mason had barely enough money to keep herself and Rob, the only child left at home. Will insisted on helping all they could.

Trinity never forgot her mother's tear-stained face, surrounded by a wreath of white hair, when she poured out her heart. "It's so terrible. Every month a rude, demanding letter comes from the undertaker. He knows I'm paying everything I can! I've even dreamed that Edmund returned and confronted the man, demanding that he stop persecuting us."

Yet somehow they lived through it all. If Trinity's torch of hope flickered and almost went out, knowledge it had been lit and placed in her hands by God kept her from total despair. Even when they could no longer make payments on their home and forty acres now under cultivation, the belief that God would never forsake them upheld her—and Will.

"I'll go see Pa," Will said when he told her the bad news.

Her mind flicked back. The very predictableness of Will's response offered security.

A month later, Will and his family moved their remaining possessions into their new home, the White Rock School in which Trinity had once taught! Situated on land donated by Pa Thatcher years before, the building belonged to him as well. When the schools consolidated and forced all students to attend school in Cedar Ridge, the building had reverted back to the Thatchers. Pa remodeled the one-room school into a huge kitchen and dining room. The old cloak room became a bedroom and he built on a living room and two more bedrooms, plus a wide front and small back porch. The two acres had sandy soil, stumps, and rocks. Subject to vandalism from standing empty it also had broken glass. Trinity raked and Will hauled away loads of debris to make the new place safe. Candleshine pulled weeds and rejoiced. This home was much closer to Jamie, Charity, Bruce, and his stepbrother and stepsister who had completed their family.

One evening when Trinity felt even her bones would protest if she took one more step, Will found her curled in an old chair on the porch. The sounds of Bruce and Candleshine's voices drifted out from a game they played at the kitchen table.

Will silently dropped to another chair and let himself relax. Nightbirds cried mournfully as the first star came out, then another. "Well, one thing about it. When things hit bedrock, the only place they can go is up."

Trinity looked into the now-spangled sky and reached for his hand. "I know. One of these days something wonderful will happen. I've been feeling it for a long time." She tightened her hold, feeling the calluses formed by the many garden hours she had spent to save Will from extra work.

"I hope so." Will closed his eyes. A few minutes later his hand fell from Trinity's and she realized he had fallen asleep. With a tender smile she slipped into the house for a worn blanket and covered him then returned to her chair to keep vigil in the soft night air.

Threads of silver glinted in Will's tossed hair, Trinity observed, as once again her heart swelled with gratitude for his relentless devotion. Once in a long time she thought of John Standish and his proposal that seemed a century ago. Most likely his wheat kingdom had survived. Still, the kingdom he'd offered could not compare with her own humble domain.

A few weeks later, Will burst in looking younger than he had in years. "I've got a job. A real, pay-for-sure job!" He caught his wife and did his own version of the Highland fling.

Breathless and laughing, Trinity demanded, "Where? How?"

"The WPA* started by President Roosevelt is going to build a new high school in Cedar Ridge. I've been hired as a laborer to haul concrete. A regular paycheck instead of a few dollars here and there! Why, you can buy silk dresses and plan a trip to Europe and—"

"Don't be silly, Daddy." Candleshine appeared in the doorway. "We'll just be glad for you to have a good job." Her lake-blue eyes shone.

---

*Works Progress (later, Work Projects) Administration.

But a week later Will trudged in with steps heavier than concrete. He washed up and ate supper in silence. When Trinity began to clean up, he spoke in a low, soft voice. "I may lose my job."

Trinity's hands stilled in her soapy dishwater. "Why?" His look of despair sent a shaft of pain to her heart.

"The foreman ordered me today to water down the concrete."

"I don't understand." She dried her hands and knelt in front of the same kitchen rocking chair that once graced the Doll House.

"Strong concrete calls for a certain percentage of cement which is the fine, gray powder that mixes with water into a bonding material when added to sand and crushed gravel." His troubled eyes looked straight into hers. "If you don't mix it properly, the final product won't wear right. I overheard the foreman talking with one of the men. Seems the more he can keep the cost down, the better job he will be given later."

"But you can't mix concrete that won't hold up," she protested. "Why, it could be unsafe! What if an earthquake came?"

"I need the job, God knows how much." He stood. "Trinity, you'll back me in what I have to do?" He lifted her to her feet.

She bit her lip. In a way it wasn't *his* responsibility. He had to follow orders. But on the other hand . . . .

"I don't think I need any job badly enough to compromise what I believe."

The same integrity she'd seen in the bewildered young married man who expected others to live by his inflexible honor reflected in his eyes. "You must do what is right, no matter what happens."

"Thanks, dear one." He kissed her and walked to the door. "Don't wait up if I'm late. I need to think." Yet the sound of his footsteps going out the door and across the porch little resembled the plodding ones when he came home from work.

Will walked across stump-dotted fields, past Trinity's garden, and through neighboring land toward the river bottoms. Cottonwoods swished and willows whispered. Tall grass bent beneath his light steps. When he reached a cherished spot that gave him a view of the river, the valley, and the protecting mountains, he leaned against a tree.

"Well, God, the way I see it I don't have a choice. You know how happy I was to get the job, but I can't go along with cheap work. Maybe You let me have the job so I could stop something bad happening by speaking up." He raised his stern face to the cloud-clotted sky and hunched hills. "It isn't just Trinity who's supposed to carry Your torch. Now it's my turn."

Hours later he returned, quietly undressed, and slipped into bed.

A soft voice said, "There was never any doubt, was there?"

Glad that she'd stayed awake, he whispered, "No," and knew how truly he spoke. "I'll talk to the head man tomorrow—and look for another job the day after."

Trinity giggled. "Don't forget, when we serve God we're never out of work!"

He grinned in the darkness and agreed.

Trinity expected Will home shortly after he reached Cedar Ridge the next day. But the kitchen clock slowly ticked off minutes then hours. Maybe the head man hadn't been on the job. Maybe Will couldn't get him aside and report what was happening. Or—Trinity flinched. Would the foreman retaliate? She finally decided Will had simply given his report and gone out to hunt a new job so she prepared the best supper she could. He'd make sure to be home at the usual time.

Promptly at five-thirty Will marched in the door, grabbed a pan, and poured in hot water to wash. He kept his head down while he muttered, "Well, I'm no longer a laborer."

She had expected it but Trinity still caught back a sigh. "What happened?"

Will soaped and splashed his face then buried it in the folds of a towel. "First thing this morning I told the foreman I couldn't accept his orders. He fired me on the spot." He toweled briskly. "I grabbed my jacket and started to walk away after I told him if he didn't tell the supervisor about making inferior concrete I would. He started yelling and swearing it was none of my business."

Trinity held her breath.

Will's cheeks were pink. "I told him it was every man's business to protect young people's lives. About then the supervisor came tearing up.

" 'What the blue blazes is going on here?' he yelled.

" 'Thatcher refuses to take orders,' the foreman yelled back.

" 'How come? What orders? He's been here all week and knows what to do. Why does he need new orders?' "

Will's eyes started to shine. "The supervisor turned to me. 'What's he talking about?'

" 'Ask him,' I said, and the supervisor's gaze bored

into the foreman.

" 'Beggin' your pardon, Boss, but he's tryin' to get Thatcher to water down the concrete,' one of the builders called.

" '*What*?' I never heard such cussing as I heard from the supervisor." Will couldn't contain his glee. "The foreman couldn't get in one word in his own defense." He threw down the towel and doubled over laughing.

"I don't understand," Trinity told him when he stopped laughing enough to hear. "You said this happened early this morning. Where have you been all day?"

"Working."

"*Working*! Will, you told me you were no longer a laborer." How could he joke, or had he really found another job so soon? God could certainly make a door and open it when needed.

"I'm not a laborer, I'm a *foreman*," Will declared proudly.

Trinity's knees gave way. She dropped into the kitchen rocker and wordlessly demanded an explanation of his crazy behavior.

"Trinity, darling girl, the supervisor had a lot to say about expecting honest work and needing men who weren't afraid to do it. He said he wanted people he could trust when he couldn't be around to check everything out. Then he said, polite as can be, 'Mr. Thatcher, I'd be proud to hire you as foreman for this job. The pay's ten dollars a month more.'

"So I said, just as politely, 'Thanks, Boss. Shall I start now?' " Suddenly the boisterous gladness faded. "I knew God would take care of us but I didn't know how quick He'd do it!"

For the rest of the 1930s Will had work from jobs offered on the strong recommendation of the WPA supervisor.

On a cloudless late spring day in 1938 a little group of Cedar Ridge men visited Trinity while Will was at work. The spokesman of the group went right to the point.

"Mrs. Thatcher, we desperately need you. Now that things are a mite better, folks are pouring into Cedar Ridge bringing their kids. The fact is, we don't have enough teachers and can't get enough good ones. Will you teach in Cedar Ridge next fall? Now that your gal's grown, isn't it time you considered going back to teaching?"

Trinity's brain whirled. She hadn't thought of teaching for a long time. Home and family had kept her busy but what he said was true. Bruce had long since left her care and was in Seattle studying medicine. Candleshine, faithful as ever, declared if he meant to be a doctor, then she'd be a nurse. When Trinity gently tried to persuade her to go into teaching, and shared how Grandma Clarissa had passed on the torch of responsibility to others, Candleshine's eyes glowed.

"Mother, I'll carry the torch! Think of Florence Nightingale, the lady of the lamp. Why, the beams from her light have spread into some of the darkest corners. I can hardly wait to get started."

"She's right," Will chimed in, and Trinity found her eyes wet. She put her hands on Candleshine's shoulders and looked deep into the beautiful, earnest eyes. "Then be the best nurse anywhere," she whispered.

"Well, Mrs. Thatcher, will you at least talk it over with your husband?"

Her visitor's voice brought Trinity back to the present.

"Of course." But she still felt dazed when they left, wondering why she hadn't simply said no.

That night after supper she and Will walked down to the river. Trinity stopped to touch a wildflower. "Will, the Cedar Ridge school board visited me today. They want me to teach for them starting in the fall."

He solemnly stared at her, his eyes thoughtful. "Aren't we getting along all right without you having to work?"

She smiled at his initial reaction.

"Aren't you happy at home?"

"No one could be happier." Her lips trembled. "But Will, with Candleshine going away for nurses' training soon, I honestly don't know if I have enough to do to keep me busy now that it will be just the two of us."

Will understood at once. "And even worse, with me gone all day, it's going to be pretty lonesome—not like knowing Candleshine will be home from school in the middle of the afternoon. If you'll be happier, it's fine with me."

"Thank you," Trinity whispered, and leaned against his strength, passionately wishing to hold this moment forever. A combination of expectancy and fear clutched her. It had been years since she'd taught and now instead of all eight grades in a one-room school, she'd teach a combination room of top sixth and seventh graders. She'd need to catch up on changes in education, perhaps take summer school courses in Bellingham. Yet the school board had said not to let modern methods change her own skilled teaching of reading, writing, and arithmetic.

Trinity closed her eyes. This time when she boarded the train for Bellingham, even if only for a month's summer school, would she be better prepared to leave her family than she had been in 1912? What if something happened to Will? Could she stand not being there when he came home from work every night, his blue eyes telling her how much more he loved her?

The unfamiliar verse she had found long ago and made her own whispered in her ears. *For thou wilt light my candle: the Lord my God will enlighten my darkness.* (Psalm 18:28).

If ever the world needed more light it was now. She and Will had studied the rise of the godless dictator, Adolf Hitler. His ruthless motto, "Close your eyes to pity! Act brutally," even now prepared young men for the destruction that must inevitably follow. How could Trinity sit in her cozy home when American young people desperately needed to be taught the values on which their country must stand?

Yes, she must again lift high her torch. Trinity squared her shoulders, breathed a prayer, and surrendered to the future, upheld by Will's love and God's beckoning, cradling hand.

A Letter To Our Readers

Dear Readers:

In order that we might better contribute to your reading enjoyment, we would appreciate your taking a few minutes to respond to the following questions and return to:

Editor
Heartsong Presents
P.O. Box 719
Uhrichsville, Ohio 44683

1. Did you enjoy reading *A Torch For Trinity*?
   - ❏ Very much. I would like to see more books by this author!
   - ❏ Moderately
   - ❏ I would have enjoyed it more if

   _____

2. Where did you purchase this book?_____

   _____

3. What influenced your decision to purchase this book?
   - ❏ Cover   ❏ Back cover copy
   - ❏ Title   ❏ Friends
   - ❏ Publicity   ❏ Other _____

4. Please rate the following elements from 1 (poor) to 10 (superior).

- ❏ Heroine
- ❏ Hero
- ❏ Setting
- ❏ Plot
- ❏ Inspirational theme
- ❏ Secondary characters

5. What settings would you like to see in Heartsong Presents Books?

_____

_____

6. What are some inspirational themes you would like to see treated in future books?

_____

_____

7. Would you be interested in reading other Heartsong Presents books?

- ❏ Very interested
- ❏ Moderately interested
- ❏ Not interested

8. Please indicate your age:

- ❏ Under 18
- ❏ 18-24
- ❏ 25-34
- ❏ 35-45
- ❏ 46-55
- ❏ Over 55

Name _____

Occupation _____

Address _____

City_____ State _____ Zip _____

HAVE YOU MISSED ANY OF THESE TITLES?

These additional titles in our Romance Reader series contain two complete romance novels for the price of one. You'll enjoy hours of great inspirational reading. Published at $7.95 each, these titles are available through Heartsong Presents for $3.97 each.

_____ RR2 A MIGHTY FLAME &
         A CHANGE OF HEART *by Irene Brand*

_____ RR3 LEXI'S NATURE &
         TORI'S MASQUERADE *by Eilene M. Berger*

_____ RR5 SONG OF JOY &
         ECHOES OF LOVE *by Elaine Schulte*

_____ RR7 FOR LOVE ALONE &
         LOVE'S SWEET PROMISE *by Susan Feldhake*

_____ RR9 SUMMER'S WIND BLOWING &
         SPRING WATERS RUSHING *by Susannah Hayden*

_____ RR10 SECOND SPRING &
          THE KISS GOODBYE *by Sally Laity*

Send to: Heartsong Presents Reader's Service
P.O. Box 719
Uhrichsville, Ohio 44683

Please send me the items checked above. I am enclosing
$_____(please add $1.00 to cover postage and handling).
Send check or money order, no cash or C.O.D.s, please.
To place a credit card order, call 1-800-847-8270.

NAME _____

ADDRESS _____

CITY / STATE _____ ZIP_____
RR

LOVE A GREAT LOVE STORY?

Introducing Heartsong Presents —
Your Inspirational Book Club

Heartsong Presents Christian romance reader's service will provide you with four never before published romance titles each month! In fact, your books will be mailed to you at the same time advance copies are sent to book reviewers. You'll preview each of these new and unabridged books before they are released to the general public.

These books are filled with the kind of stories you have been longing for—stories of courtship, chivalry, honor, and virtue. Strong characters and riveting plot lines will make you want to read on and on. Romance is not dead, and each of these romantic tales will remind you that Christian faith is still the vital ingredient in an intimate relationship filled with true love and honest devotion.

Sign up today to receive your first set. Send no money now. We'll bill you only $9.97 post-paid with your shipment. Then every month you'll automatically receive the latest four "hot off the press" titles for the same low post-paid price of $9.97. That's a savings of 50% off the $4.95 cover price. When you consider the exaggerated shipping charges of other book clubs, your savings are even greater!

THERE IS NO RISK—you may cancel at any time without obligation. And if you aren't completely satisfied with any selection, return it for an immediate refund.

TO JOIN, just complete the coupon below, mail it today, and get ready for hours of wholesome entertainment every month.

Now you can curl up, relax, and enjoy some great reading full of the warmhearted spirit of romance.

---------- Curl up with Heartsong! ----------

YES! Sign me up for Heartsong!

FIRST SET TO SHIP OCTOBER 15, 1992.
Orders received after that date will be shipped immediately!
Send no money now. We'll bill you only $9.97 post-paid with your first shipment of four books.

NAME _____

ADDRESS _____

CITY _____ STATE / ZIP _____
MAIL TO: HEARTSONG / P.O. Box 719 Uhrichsville, Ohio 44683
YES